ALMOST SISTERS
THE SISTERS SCHEME

KATHRYN MAKRIS is the author of a number of books for young adults, some of which have been translated into Spanish, Italian, French, and German. She also works as a reporter and has published articles in *Mother Jones* magazine, the San Francisco *Chronicle*, and other publications. Her interview credits include the Reverend Jesse Jackson, Ralph Nader, Gloria Steinem, Sissy Spacek, Ted Danson, "Colonel" Sanders, and Benji the dog. The ALMOST SISTERS trilogy are her first books for middle grade readers.

She enjoys hiking, swimming, nature study, and travel, migrating regularly between California and the state she grew up in, Texas.

ALMOST SISTERS
THE SISTERS SCHEME

KATHRYN MAKRIS

AN AVON CAMELOT BOOK

THE SISTERS SCHEME is an original publication of Avon Books. This work has
never before appeared in book form.

AVON BOOKS
A division of
The Hearst Corporation
1350 Avenue of the Americas
New York, New York 10019

This series is dedicated to one of the best things around—friendship—and to my friends, some of the best around.

For special help on this book, thanks to Meg, Sharon, Ricky G., Lynn, and Gavin.

Thanks also to the National Women Composers Resource Center in San Francisco and to cellist Stephen Harrison.

Chapter 1

Vanessa Shepherd leaned against the trunk of a fat, old oak tree next to her best friend, Ricki Romero.

"I can't believe he's going to make me live here," Vanessa mumbled shakily.

The two girls gazed at a sad-looking house. Faded, peeling gray paint, boarded-up windows, a sagging roof, and a lopsided porch.

"There's just no way it will be ready by Christmas, like Dad says." Vanessa fanned herself miserably against the August heat with the hem of her cotton blouse.

The heat almost took her mind off the house. That was just one of the many differences between her and Ricki, who soaked up summer as happily as a sunflower. Tall, athletic Ricki, with naturally bronze skin that hardly ever burned and a big, contagious smile.

The screech of an electric drill came from what Vanessa's father called the kitchen.

"Hey, this place isn't so bad, Vee. I think it's going to be great." Ricki aimed her new camera at the house and snapped the shutter. "I mean, with a few good nails in the right places."

She bit her lip and nudged her blue baseball cap back. If there was one thing Ricki couldn't stand, it was seeing Vanessa sad. The sight of those gentle green eyes clouding

1

up tempted her to stand on her head, tell silly jokes, do anything to help cheer up her friend.

"I don't understand why we can't stay in the duplex," Vanessa said, her voice growing a little more steady. Having Ricki beside her always made things seem better. "We're just fine there."

Ricki nodded. Vanessa and her father, Andy, had been living in the duplex apartment above a nice old woman named Mrs. Quan when she and Vanessa met three years ago in third grade, and even before that.

"Now how did your dad get this place?" Ricki asked, noticing that Vanessa's small, slender shoulders were slumping a little less. "Somebody just gave it to him?"

"Practically." Vanessa pushed blond bangs away from her steaming forehead. "One of his music students inherited it, but he's already rich and didn't want to take the trouble to fix it up. He just asked Dad how much he could afford to pay and sold it to him."

"Just like that?" Ricki exclaimed. "A whole house?"

Vanessa pursed her lips. "This house. That's not saying much."

Ricki used one of her long black pigtails to hide her grin. It was funny to hear even-tempered Vanessa get sarcastic for a change, and it was a lot better than seeing her sad.

The drill noise was suddenly drowned by a radio blasting out music.

Vanessa saw Ricki's lips move but couldn't hear her. "What?"

"I said," Ricki yelled, "that it's a good thing your neighbors here aren't too close!" The music toned down in the middle of Ricki's sentence so that her last words came out as a shout.

From the kitchen Vanessa's father yelled, "Talking to me?"

"I said—" Ricki began again.

Vanessa interrupted. "Wait. The neighbors aren't that far away."

The girls waded through a jungle of weeds to get to the kitchen window, just a gap in the boards that Andy had sawed through.

Vanessa and Ricki stood on their tiptoes to watch him lift a rusty sink out of its frame and set it on the floor. He groaned.

Vanessa heard Ricki's camera clicking.

"We were just trying to talk over the music," Vanessa told her father through the boards. She tried to sound calm but was wondering what would happen if her father hurt himself while fixing up this awful house. He wasn't a very big or strong man—just average.

"Oh, sorry." Andy wiped sweat off his forehead with the sleeve of his red Talking Heads T-shirt. His shaggy, light brown hair was sopping wet. He grinned. "I turned the radio up too high. You girls doing okay? Want some more lemonade, Ricki? Made with homegrown lemons, you know. See the trees out there?"

Ricki nodded. "They're great. And I'm fine, thanks. Vanessa gave me the grand tour. Now we're just waiting for my mom."

"Good. Well, let me know when she gets here, okay? I want to say hi." He grinned again.

Ricki thought about how different and how alike Andy and Vanessa could look, depending on their moods. Andy was almost always cheerful. His ever-ready, friendly smile sometimes reminded her of a little boy's. Vanessa had that same sweet smile, but because she was on the shy side most people never saw it.

3

On her dresser Vanessa kept a picture of her mother, Celeste. Ricki had never met Vanessa's mother, because Celeste and Andy had been divorced since Vanessa was four, and she traveled around on singing jobs. Even Vanessa rarely saw her. But from the picture, Ricki could see that Vanessa definitely took after her petite, pretty mother. They both looked like the delicate elf princesses in fairy-tale books.

She followed Vanessa on the path that led to the backyard. Untrimmed bushes tangled in the border beds, brightened by a few yellow dandelions and orange California poppies.

"Maybe one reason your dad likes it here is because he can make a lot more noise than he can at the duplex and not bother anyone. I mean, with his guitar and his rock band and everything."

Up ahead, Vanessa's shoulder-length ponytail bobbed in a nod. "I know. I think that was his main reason for buying this place."

"Here you can practice your cello anytime you want, without worrying about Mrs. Quan," Ricki offered cheerfully.

"I'm used to worrying about Mrs. Quan."

"And you won't have to listen to the little kids she takes care of while you're trying to do your homework," Ricki added.

"I'm used to the little kids."

"You'll get used to this, too, Vee. It's a great place. Room to spread out. A front yard, backyard, trees, flowers. Didn't your dad even say you could get a dog after you move in?"

Another bob of the ponytail.

"See? You want a dog. All you have now is goldfish!" Ricki still felt bad for Vanessa, who must really be upset

4

to complain so much. Usually Vanessa was pretty easy-going about things. But she sure could be stubborn sometimes.

Vanessa pulled the rusted latch on a little wooden gate and let them through.

"Oh, wow!" Ricki's ink black eyes sparkled even more than usual. "Now this is a backyard!" She took another picture.

"But it's all weeds!" Vanessa protested.

It was mostly weeds, Ricki agreed silently. But under the weeds the land sloped gently upward to a wooden fence at the top of the hill. Trees dappled it all over—fruit trees and some old, interesting oaks like the ones in the front yard.

Vanessa trudged uphill through the weeds behind Ricki, thinking that they would probably pick up ticks. And ants. Or even scorpions or something. They had almost reached the fence when she asked, "Are there scorpions in California?"

"Yeah, I think so," Ricki answered.

"What if we find one?"

"Oh, Vee." Ricki rolled her eyes. "What would a scorpion be doing here, in the middle of Berkeley? You're the big nature freak. You should know."

"Ouch!" Vanessa yelped.

Ricki turned. "What?"

"A burr on my sock."

"Well, pick it off." Ricki had only so much patience, even for her best friend. "Honestly, Vee. You have to make an effort."

"I am. This hill is an effort." She frowned.

"I mean about the house. You're stuck with it. Your father is not going to change his mind. At least give it a chance."

5

"But I like it at Mrs. Quan's." Vanessa knew she sounded like a whiny baby. Was it too much to ask just to stay in one place—all settled in? To not move into a house that might collapse?

"I wouldn't mind living here. The place has possibilities."

Vanessa sighed and looked down at the weeds. "Oh, Ricki. I wish you *could* live here. That's the only thing that would make it bearable, if we could live here together."

"And have breakfast together every day." Ricki grinned.

"And ride to school together," added Vanessa.

"Then ride home together."

"Be together all we wanted!"

Both girls smiled happily, standing thigh-high in the weeds and chattering about one of their favorite dreams.

The first time they'd thought of it had been two years before, when Ricki made friends with the Murdoch twins. They watched the twins talk alike, walk alike, dress alike, go everywhere together, and never be apart. Back then they realized how great it would be to be twins—or even just sisters. How it would mean never having to be alone again, or lonely, or be the only child and only target of your mom's or dad's worrying and griping.

The honk of a car horn interrupted their daydream.

"My mom," Ricki said with a sigh.

Vanessa sighed, too. "One of us always has to go home."

"I know." Ricki made a face.

The two of them hiked back downhill to the front yard, where they saw Andy walking toward Ricki's mom, Anita, at the curb.

"Oh, she always looks so pretty," said Vanessa.

Tall, slender Anita came around her car to meet Andy with her usual brisk walk.

"Yeah." Ricki nodded proudly. "We call that red dress her 'Saturday suit.' It's what she wears when she has to work on Saturday. Wait. I'll take a picture of her."

"Would you want a job like hers? A . . . what is it? Investments advisor? So you could tell people how to spend their money?"

"Nah," Ricki answered. "Mostly Mom tells them how to save it, and that would be boring. Plus she has to wear nylons every day."

"Yuck." Vanessa wrinkled her nose.

The girls waited while their parents exchanged hellos.

Anita slipped her arm around Ricki's shoulders. "Well, we'd better get going, honey."

Ricki looked up at her. "You got your hair done."

"Ah, I thought I noticed something different," Andy said, stroking his short brown beard. "Looks nice."

Ricki wasn't sure, but she thought she noticed her mom's high, rosy-brown cheekbones getting a little rosier.

"Well, thank you." Anita fumbled with a dark curl that was straying out of her new swept-back style.

"Couldn't Ricki stay longer?" Vanessa pleaded, just as one or the other of them always did when it was time to go.

"Not today, hon," Anita answered. "Lots of errands to run."

"Then can Vee come with us?" Ricki begged.

Andy shook his head, smiling with his friendly brown eyes. "You two are pretty predictable, you know that? You never part without a fuss. Sorry, girls, but I need Vanessa around here today."

Vanessa and Ricki sighed loudly.

"How is the house remodeling going?" Anita asked Andy.

"Remodeling? You mean rebuilding, don't you?" He laughed.

Anita laughed, too, and pretty soon they were talking about plumbing and termites and floor tile. The girls sneaked away.

"They're going to be yakking for at least another ten minutes," Ricki said. "Let's climb a tree."

"Do we have to?" Vanessa could feel her blouse clinging to her back. She was thinking about looking for a garden hose.

"Oh, come on. This one's perfect," Ricki urged, picking one of the branchy, twisted oaks nearby.

She made her way up first, camera dangling from her neck. A squirrel chattered at them from somewhere above.

"Isn't this great?" Ricki asked as they settled on a couple of branches about fifteen feet up. "Let's play pretend."

Vanessa was having trouble finding a comfortable spot on her branch. It had knobs all over it. "Pretend what?"

Ricki leaned back against the trunk, hands behind her head. "We're sisters. We both live here. Our parents are inside making dinner. Neither of us has to go home, 'cause we are home."

Vanessa finally managed to straddle her branch and hang on. "If you lived here," she said in a deep, radio announcer's voice, "you'd be home now."

"Huh?" Ricki peered around the trunk at her.

"You know, that billboard on the freeway next to those apartments?" Vanessa explained. Then she frowned. "But it's hard to pretend that we're home now, because our parents are down there talking about how awful this house is."

8

"No, they're not," Ricki disagreed. "They're talking about what awful shape it's in. There's a difference."

Anita's voice drifted up to them. "I realize it was a tough decision, Andy. But I don't think you'll regret this purchase."

Andy grinned at her. "I hope you're right."

Me, too, thought Vanessa. Underneath all her complaints, she really wanted things to work out. She wanted the house to be fixable and for her father and her to live there happily. But she didn't see how any of that was possible. She wished their lives could have just stayed calm and comfortable, the way they were.

"In fact, Anita," her father was saying, "I'm sure you're right. And I want to thank you again for your advice on the loan."

"Oh, it was nothing." Anita shrugged a shoulder.

Vanessa leaned forward.

"No, I couldn't have done it without you," Andy went on.

"Ricki," Vanessa whispered. "Did you hear that? My father is thanking your mother for advice she gave him about buying this house."

"So?"

"That means that he asked everyone in the whole world about buying it but me!" Vanessa blurted.

"My mom is not 'everyone,' Vee. It's her job to give advice about stuff like that. Plus, they're friends."

"But I'm his daughter! I'm the one who'll have to live here!"

"That's true," Ricki agreed. She sympathized with Vanessa. People have a right to say where they're going to live. But Ricki's father had died when she was three, and ever since then she and her mom had moved so many times that she had grown used to it.

"Well," she heard her mother saying, "you've come to my rescue before, too, Andy. Remember when my friend Gina was trying to find musicians at the last minute for her niece's wedding?"

"I remember." Andy nodded.

Ricki saw him look up at tall Anita and smile. Anita smiled back. A very soft smile.

Suddenly Ricki felt guilty about eavesdropping. Well, it wasn't exactly eavesdropping because their parents had seen them go up the tree and must realize they were still up there within earshot, but . . .

"Ricki," Vanessa whispered.

"Yeah?"

"Did you . . . ?"

"What?"

Both girls' eyes were glued on their parents.

"Did you see that?" Vanessa asked.

The adults went back to chatting again. The girls weren't really listening anymore. Vanessa thought of a book she had read where a man and a woman fall in love, then stand and gaze into each other's eyes. And Ricki thought of a movie she had seen, where a man and a woman fall in love, then stand and gaze into each other's eyes.

"Ricki!" Anita's voice broke through Ricki's thoughts so suddenly that she lost her balance and had to grab onto a branch to keep from falling. "How did you get up there?"

"Isn't that kind of high?" Andy chimed in.

"You saw us come up," Vanessa called.

"And you didn't tell us not to," Ricki added.

Anita planted her hands on her hips. "Well, just come down."

The girls scrambled to the ground and dusted off their

shorts. Their parents had started talking again, but Ricki and Vanessa still weren't really listening. They were looking at each other, grinning ear to ear and thinking exactly the same thing.

Chapter 2

"So you noticed it, too?" Vanessa whispered into the telephone Sunday afternoon.

"Of course I did," Ricki answered. "Who could have missed it? I should have taken a picture of them."

Both girls felt so excited they could hardly stop giggling. This was the first chance they'd had to talk to each other since Saturday afternoon. A whole day.

"They're in love," Ricki whispered.

Vanessa held her breath. "Do you really think so?"

"Well, you saw them," said Ricki. "Just like in the movies."

"Or in *Sammie's Sixteenth Summer*." Vanessa went to the door of her room and shut it softly. Her father was just down the hall, working on one of his music compositions.

Ricki shrugged. "I never saw that."

"It's not a movie, Ricki. It's a book. The eyes of the heroine and her boyfriend lock before their lips meet in a kiss."

"That sounds gross."

"I know, but that's what our parents reminded me of."

"Then you think so, too? That they're in love?" Ricki rose from her bed to shut the door of her room. Her mother was all the way downstairs in the kitchen, but you couldn't be too careful.

"Well, maybe they're . . . thinking about being in love."

"People don't think about it," Ricki scoffed. "Either they are or they aren't."

"Sure they do." Vanessa curled into her old white wicker rocker. "I mean, when they're kind of on the way to being in love."

"I guess so." Ricki shrugged.

"You do realize what this means, don't you?" Vanessa asked.

"Tell me what you're thinking." Ricki dropped back down on her unmade bed, sinking into the nest of zebra-striped sheets.

"Well, if your mother and my father—"

"We'd be sisters!" Ricki burst out. "If they ended up married."

"It seems so perfect. Your mother, a widow. My father, divorced. You and me, best friends. A perfect match!" Vanessa hugged her knees.

"Maybe they'll start dating," Ricki offered.

"Do you really think they might?"

"Why not?" Ricki stretched a long leg up into a shaft of sunlight and wiggled her toes. "You just said they're a perfect match."

"Well, they are. I mean, they're both really nice. And smart. But . . ." Vanessa picked at lint on the green chair cushion.

"Our parents are pretty different," Ricki finished for her.

"Mmm-hmm. Your mother is older than my father, isn't she? He's thirty-four."

"She's thirty-nine," Ricki said. "But that's only five years. By the time you get that old you don't notice. But she is taller."

"Just a couple of inches. Height only matters in the movies."

"True." Ricki stretched her other leg to the window and rested her foot on the sun-warmed glass. "But my mom is so hyper, always on the go, and your dad is so . . ."

"Mellow. I know." Vanessa frowned. "And your mother doesn't like rock music, does she?"

"Sure she does. But maybe not the weird kind your dad's band has been playing. What do you call it?"

"Jazz-rock? Fusion?"

"Yeah. That." Ricki was always amazed at the big words and important things Vanessa knew about. "Hey, there's another difference, too. I never see your dad reading *The Wall Street Journal*. Mom practically eats it with her coffee every morning."

Vanessa sighed. "Dad doesn't even drink coffee. Maybe it's not the perfect match."

"When is anything ever perfect, Vee? I think they just need a little . . . help."

"A push," Vanessa agreed, "in the right direction."

"Yeah, like—"

"Matchmakers. That's what they need," Vanessa said.

Ricki started giggling. Then Vanessa did.

Ricki managed to sputter, "You mean, like us!"

"Imagine, to actually be sisters! It would be so much fun!"

"There's a long way to go before that," Ricki pointed out. "I mean, there could be obstacles. Is your dad dating anyone now?"

"Not that I know of," Vanessa replied. "Not since he and Jocelyn broke up last year."

"Oh, yeah. I remember her. The ballet dancer. Kind of spacey. Well, Mom isn't dating anyone, either, since she broke up with that Eric guy at the beginning of the year. Thank goodness.''

"He was so stuck up," Vanessa observed.

"I know." Ricki scrunched up her nose. "Remember when he took us for a ride in his Porsche and kept explaining exactly how much it cost and why?"

"How could I forget?" Vanessa said. "My father would never do a thing like that. Well, I guess he couldn't afford a Porsche, either."

"I love your dad," Ricki said.

"I love your mother," said Vanessa.

"They've just got to get together." Ricki let her legs drop to the bed with a thud.

"Right." Vanessa raised an eyebrow. "And I've got an idea."

"Yeah?" Rick sat up.

"Let's test them out. I mean, find out how they feel."

"About what?"

"Each other, of course," said Vanessa.

"Hmm." Ricki tapped a finger on her cheek. "But in a subtle way, right? So they'll never guess. We can't tell anyone what we're doing. It would scare our parents off if they found out."

"You're right," said Vanessa. "They're both so stubborn."

"See? They do have something in common."

Vanessa laughed. "They both like to tell us what to do, too."

"And make us get off the phone," said Ricki.

"And never listen to reason," said Vanessa.

"A perfect match!" Ricki nodded.

"Perfect," Vanessa agreed.

"And you and I, Vee, are going to make it happen."

*   *   *

15

Ricki flung open the freezer door, which was black. She had never seen a black freezer, or black oven or refrigerator or dishwasher, before she and her mother moved into the condo a year ago. For that matter, she had never seen a dishwasher at all except at Uncle Mario and Aunt Ruth's house in nearby Hayward. But they were practically rich because of Uncle Mario's Mexican deli shop.

Ricki and her mother had never been rich, but things were going a lot better these days. And living in the all-modern condo made Ricki feel rich sometimes.

She pulled out two frozen lasagna dinners and set them on the black countertop. Everything in the kitchen was either black or white or stainless steel. "A sleek, clean look," the man who rented her mom the condo had said.

Mom loved it. So did Ricki. The kitchen and the rest of the place were like something you'd see on "Star Trek," all push-button and automatic, ready to take off at any minute.

Ricki unwrapped the dinner platters, popped them into the black microwave, and beeped the timer on.

One of her favorite things about Mondays was getting to choose whatever she wanted for dinner. Her mother always got home an hour late that night and on Thursdays because of meetings. So it was Ricki's job to get dinner started. Other nights, her mom came home and cooked. In the old days, when Anita was still in college and working, too, they got to eat frozen dinners almost every night. Now her mom was on a sort of cooking kick. Most of it still involved heavy use of the microwave, but she had read somewhere about the importance of vegetables.

Oh, well, Ricki thought. A few vegetables probably never hurt anybody. At least not fatally. And as far as tonight's menu went, Ricki had a few items of her own to add to it. That is, a few carefully selected questions about her mother's attitude toward a certain person. A certain Mr. Andy Shepherd.

Ricki grinned, then checked the sink for dirty dishes. Only half full. She and her mom never bothered with dishes until they buried the sink and adjacent countertops. Rummaging around in the cupboard, Ricki found a box of chocolate chip cookies. She shoved a pile of junk mail off a barstool, climbed onto it, and opened the newspaper to the comics.

Her mother came home in the middle of *Calvin and Hobbes*. Her heels came clicking on the hall floor toward the kitchen.

"Well, hello, sweetie," she said, bustling up to the counter with an armload of paper sacks.

"Hi. What's that?" Ricki rested her chin on a hand.

"Groceries," her mom replied, planting a kiss on Ricki's head.

"But I already cooked."

"They're for other days. Frozen peas and things."

"Oh." Ricki finished the last bite of her cookie.

"Honey," her mother said.

"Hmm?" Ricki noticed her mom had stopped in the middle of unloading the groceries and was staring at her, dark eyes squinting.

"What are you eating?"

"Cookies," Ricki answered.

"I see that. Before dinner?" Her mother's black eyebrows lowered.

"I was hungry."

Anita threw her hands in the air. "It's hopeless."

"What is?" Ricki asked.

Her mom went back to stuffing plastic packages into the freezer. "Organizing our nutrition."

"It's organized," Ricki said. "We eat every day."

"Oh, Ricki."

"Hey, I'm healthy. Look." She shoved up the sleeve of her sweatshirt and made a muscle.

Her mom smiled. "Knock on wood. You have looked pretty chipper this summer. What did you do today?"

"In the morning I watched 'Bewitched' and 'Wheel of Fortune.' "

Anita rolled her eyes. "Too much TV."

"Then I played soccer in the courtyard with the Steinberg kids from across the hall," Ricki went on. "And I took some pictures of the condo. Then I went downstairs to the drugstore to pick up my pictures of Vanessa and Andy's new house."

Ricki's mom put a hand on her hip. The other hand held one of the lasagna dinner platters in an oven mitt. She set it in front of Ricki. "More pictures?"

Ricki bit at a thumbnail. "Just one roll."

"Hon, we can't afford this. That credit card I gave you is for emergencies only. You're using it like it's just a piece of plastic."

"Only on my photos, Mom. I never buy anything else."

"Your allowance is not enough to cover all the film and processing you've been getting, Ricki. You have to budget."

"I do budget," Ricki protested. "I only shoot three rolls a week."

"Honey, that's over a hundred pictures, isn't it? Uncle Mario told you to practice when he gave you that camera for your birthday—not to photograph everything in sight!"

"But that is how you practice, Mom. He said the way you learn is to shoot a lot of pictures."

Her mother sat on the barstool opposite Ricki. "It's true that I'm making a good living now. But we also have more expenses. The car is getting old and needs repairs

18

every few months. I decided to rent this condo because we deserved something nice, for a change, but it's not cheap. We can't spend blindly.''

"I'm not, Mom! Photography is my hobby. Maybe my career.''

"Find a less expensive one. Or cut down to one roll a week.''

"Mo-om.''

"Don't whine, Ricki. I'm just telling you the way things are.''

Ricki bunched her mouth to one side and stared at her plate. No use arguing with her mom once she got into one of her scrimp-and-save moods. Vanessa was right. Parents never listened to reason.

She took a slow, mopey bite of lasagna. Only one roll of film a week? She must be kidding. The fancy, new camera Uncle Mario had given her in June was the best present ever. She really did want to photograph everything in sight. Her mother just didn't understand.

Forget asking her any questions about Andy now. Thanks to the argument about overspending, her mom would be jumpy all night. Money problems always made her nervous. Ricki would have to wait until tomorrow to work on the scheme to become sisters with Vanessa.

It clicked. Scheme . . . Sisters . . . The Sisters Scheme!

It sounded great! She couldn't wait to tell Vanessa that their plan had a name. If only they were already sisters, Ricki thought glumly, then she wouldn't have to wait to tell Vee anything. And maybe her mother would have better things to do than yell at her.

Vanessa positioned her fingers on the neck of her cello, waiting. A light breeze stirred the leaves just outside the living room window.

Her father's friend, Gordon Taylor, broke the silence with a flurry of bright notes on the piano. Vanessa drew her bow across the strings of her instrument to make clear, rich tones. And after just a few beats, her dad joined in on his mellow-sounding acoustic guitar.

Vanessa kept her eyes on the music sheet, concentrating. She loved practicing classical music pieces with her father and Gordon. Pieces like this trio by Haydn gave her a calm, safe feeling. At that moment, sitting in the cozy living room, everything in the world seemed to be in order.

"Well, well." Andy grinned when they finished the trio.

Gordon nodded, adjusting his wire-rim glasses. "Very good."

"Really?" Vanessa asked.

Gordon's dark face lit up with a smile. "Great, in fact."

"But I stumbled a lot," Vanessa pointed out.

"Nah, not a lot," Andy said. "You played right through. This is good for me, too. I haven't been doing much classical lately."

"Keeps us in shape." Gordon winked a dark brown eye.

"Um, excuse me." A head of spiked-up blond hair poked through the kitchen doorway. "Have any baking soda?"

"Sure, Zinna," Andy replied, resting his hands on the side of his guitar. "Look on the first shelf of the cupboard above the stove."

"What's Zinna doing this time—making cookies?" Gordon muttered.

Andy grinned. "No. A collage. Fabric and cardboard and clothespins all stuck together."

"Sounds more tame than the usual stuff in progress here, like that werewolf head totem pole thing in the dining room."

Gordon liked to make fun of Andy's artist friends who used his home as a studio. But Vanessa didn't mind Zinna and the others, even if they did make a mess sometimes.

"Hey, we've all been there, you know," Andy said. "Needing a place to work. Zinna lives in a cubbyhole garage apartment."

"Andy Shepherd," Gordon said. "Friend to starving artists."

Andy gave him a friendly punch in the arm. "Come on. You two want to go through the Haydn again?"

"Tomorrow," answered Gordon. "I've got to run."

"You're not staying for dinner?" asked Vanessa. She liked Gordon. He had known her since she was a baby back in Boston.

"Thanks, but I'm picking up Suzanne. She's getting in from Egypt." Gordon pulled a khaki cap over his short-cropped black hair.

"Oh, wow!" Vanessa cried. She liked thinking about Gordon's girlfriend, Suzanne, traveling all over the world in her job as a flight attendant.

When Andy came back from seeing Gordon to the door, Vanessa was still dreaming about faraway deserts and pyramids.

"After we move into the Mariposa Lane house," Andy said, bringing Vanessa back to reality with a thud, "we won't have to worry about artists in the kitchen at dinnertime. Hey, how about some of my world-famous chicken stroganoff tonight?"

"Okay," Vanessa said, then went quiet. She didn't want to hear another word about the house tonight. She wanted to stay in a happy, dreamy mood. And then, later, she'd ask her father subtle questions about his feelings toward Ricki's mother.

But her dad seemed to have a one-track mind. "At the new house," he went on, straightening the throw pillows on the sofa, "we'll eventually build a separate art studio above the garage. The garage itself we'll make our music studio."

Vanessa carefully rested her cello on its side on the floor. "When is Zinna supposed to be finished tonight?"

"I told her she could work until six. And clean up after herself." Andy started strumming soft chords on his guitar. "Doesn't that sound great, Rainbow?" That was one of his pet names for her.

Vanessa nodded. "She made an awful mess last week."

"I know." Andy laughed. "But I meant about the studios. Doesn't that sound great?"

"Oh." Vanessa sighed quietly. "Sure."

"Vee, can't you get even a little excited about the new house?" Andy laid his guitar on the sofa and sat down next to it.

"I like it fine here."

"You've already told me that." It was Andy's turn to sigh.

"Then why don't you ever listen?" Vanessa couldn't help asking, even though she hated arguments.

Her father looked up at her. "I guess I just don't understand. It's like you think the world will fall apart if we move."

"That house might fall apart." Vanessa stared at her goldfish, Hugo and Hannah, swimming in their bowl on the end table.

Andy laughed softly. "Oh, Vee, it's not that bad. Really. I've had the house inspected, and the experts all say it's a good structure. The way it looks is the worst part.''

"There's no way you'll have it fixed by Christmas."

"I think I will. I'm getting lots of help, you know. I forgot to mention to Gordon that it's great when artists owe you favors, because most of them have pretty handy day jobs. Bernard is a carpenter; Maureen works in a garden shop. Oh, and Zinna, believe it or not, knows a lot about plumbing." He smiled happily.

"What if they don't come through? What if your friends don't have time, or if they flake out?"

"Vanessa." Andy rested his elbows on his knees. His fingers were laced together lightly, dangling toward the floor. He stared at the floor, too. It was his gearing-up position. Vanessa knew he was trying not to lose his patience. "All I ask is that you not be so negative. I'd like for you to listen to yourself."

Vanessa didn't answer. She knew she sounded negative. She *had* been listening to herself. The problem was that her father hadn't been listening to her at all. A month ago he had bought the Mariposa Lane house without telling her. Just two weeks ago he announced they'd be moving in at Christmas. And that was that.

Her father had never done anything like this before. He and Vanessa were a team, she thought. They were supposed to talk about things.

"Finished." Zinna came charging out of the kitchen, pulling on her paint-splattered denim jacket. "Gotta go. Thanks. I cleaned up." She waved and was out the front door.

Andy stood up. "Let's start dinner."

Vanessa followed him to the kitchen, although she didn't feel like dinner. She felt like calling Ricki. Ricki always listened.

23

Chapter 3

Ricki came zooming down the slide and landed in the sand with a thump. She gazed up into a sunny blue sky. If there was one thing she loved, it was summer in September.

Vanessa landed right behind her.

"Ow!" Ricki giggled, rubbing her shoulder where Vanessa's foot had whacked her on the way down.

Vanessa's bottom hurt, but she was having fun. She and Ricki hadn't played on Mrs. Quan's swing set in ages.

"Let's go again, everybody," said Ricki.

"Yes, again!" shrieked tiny, three-year-old Wilson at their heels. He and the other small children, Jessica and Paul, loved it when Ricki came over.

"Pretty soon you girls too big," Mrs. Quan said with her heavy Vietnamese accent. She sat in her lawn chair on the porch.

"Hey, we're the entertainment!" Ricki grinned at her.

Mrs. Quan waved her small hand as if there were a bug in the air, then went back to the sewing in her lap.

Ricki and Vanessa knew Mrs. Quan's grumpiness was just an act. Underneath it she was a real softie and didn't mind a bit that the girls were helping keep the kids busy.

Ricki guided Wilson up the slide's ladder while Vanessa watched. She never knew what to say to little kids or what to do when they came up and tugged on her.

24

"Don't worry," Ricki told Wilson, who always clung to her for dear life at the top of the slide. His eyes were as big as quarters. "This time Vanessa will catch you at the bottom."

"I will?" Vanessa squinted up at Ricki.

"Sure. Squat down in the sand pit. You don't really have to catch him. Just be there."

Vanessa positioned herself and waited. A squealing little bundle of boy hurtled toward her, brown hair flying. He landed right in her lap. Then he flung his tiny arms around her neck and giggled, knocking them both over into the sand.

At first Vanessa didn't know what to do, but then she laughed, too, and hugged him back. His hair smelled like fresh air.

"Watch out! Here I come!" Ricki yelled down.

Wilson and Vanessa scooted out of the way just in time.

All three sat in the sand, laughing.

"Hello, you two! Playing in the sandbox again?"

Ricki looked up and saw the Murdoch twins and their dog at the gate. "Hi! Yeah, come join in."

"We can't," Marlys said. "We're walking Murphy."

Vanessa called, "I'll walk him for you."

As soon as she opened the gate, little Murphy trotted up to her and placed both his black paws on her knee.

"Hi, Murph!" The Scottish terrier's stubby tail wagged busily when Vanessa pet him. Then he jumped off her and headed for Ricki.

"Nice doggie," Ricki said, backing up. She was not a big fan of animals. In first grade a golden retriever had dashed up to her on the sidewalk, knocked her down, and stolen her lunch. She'd been spooked about dogs ever since.

Murphy turned back to his old pal, Vanessa. She

scratched the curly black fur behind his ears. Funny, she thought, how Ricki looked the same way around Murphy as she herself must around Wilson. Maybe she should put Murphy on the slide and tell Ricki to catch him.

"Vanessa, you keep dog outside," Mrs. Quan called from the porch.

"I know, Mrs. Quan." She took the leash from Mavis and led Murphy back to the sidewalk. "Nothing personal," she told him. "Mrs. Quan just thinks you have germs. Bad for the children."

Murphy didn't seem offended. He was busy sniffing at a bush.

The twins and Ricki followed the kids back to the swing set.

Vanessa pet Murphy, glad to be walking him even though it meant missing the game. As Ricki pointed out, there was one good thing about the Mariposa Lane house: She could have her own dog there.

After about a half hour, Mavis and Marlys had to go home, and Vanessa and Ricki joined the kids on the porch for their afternoon snack. The girls leaned back in the creaky, old glider, sipping orange juice. At their feet, the little kids nibbled crackers from a low snack table.

"Mmm, this is great, Mrs. Quan," Ricki said.

"Okay. You good girls." Mrs. Quan waved a rose-printed silk fan at herself. Her wide, pleasant face hinted at a smile.

Vanessa poked an elbow at Ricki. Ricki poked back. They poked and giggled happily until Mrs. Quan told them to stop, or they'd spill their juice, and she would not be the one to clean up.

Ricki popped a cube of cheese into her mouth. She could understand why Vanessa wouldn't want to leave Mrs. Quan's. It was nice around here, kind of old-

fashioned and homey. Vanessa even stayed with Mrs.
Quan some nights when Andy had to perform with his
band. To Vanessa, whose mother was off who knew where
and whose grandparents were far away in Boston, the
duplex and Mrs. Quan had been home for years.

"Let's go up to my room," Vanessa said when they
were through munching. "We need to talk."

Ricki understood immediately. Although two weeks had
passed since they first thought up the Sisters Scheme, they
hadn't gotten anywhere yet. The start of school that week
had sidetracked them.

On the way up to the Shepherd's apartment, Ricki heard
a trumpet blaring. They opened the front door to find
Andy, Gordon, and the rest of their band, called Fast
Forward, sitting around the living room. Ricki recognized
long-haired Ike on the saxophone, skinny, blond Linda the
guitarist, Topp the trumpet man, and Paco the drummer
with dreadlocks. Andy had his electric bass guitar, and
Gordon sat at the keyboard.

"Dad and Gordon have been composing a lot of new
pieces," Vanessa whispered. "That's why they're passing
around the sheet music."

"Hello," Gordon said when he saw the girls. "How're
you, Ricki?"

"Hi. Come on in." Andy grinned, then turned back to
a conversation with Ike.

Ricki never knew how to act around Vanessa's father's
friends. They seemed so . . . unusual. And they rarely
paid much attention to her, anyway.

Vanessa, though, was looking over Topp's shoulder at
the music. "Oh, this is the one with the syncopated
rhythm," she said.

"Yeah." Topp scratched his stubbly black beard.

27

"Your daddy and his buddy get some funky ideas. What do they eat for breakfast?"

"Igor Stravinsky on toast, maybe," Vanessa said.

Topp and a couple of the others laughed.

Ricki smiled but had no idea what the joke was about. Who was Igor? Things like that were always happening at the Shepherds' apartment. Ricki hung around feeling awkward, tongue-tied, and about four years old, while Vanessa moved smoothly through conversations.

"Who," Ricki asked after they'd gone down the hall to Vanessa's room, "or what, is an Igor Str- Stra—"

"Stravinsky," Vanessa provided. "He was a Russian-American composer in the early part of the century. His style was odd and different at that time. He tried lots of new things."

"Oh." Ricki collapsed on Vanessa's old four-poster bed.

Vanessa curled up in her rocker. "Ricki, the Scheme."

"Oh, yeah." Ricki sat up. "Right. The Scheme."

"Did you ever talk to your mom?" asked Vanessa.

Ricki nodded. "She said your dad is nice."

"Nice? Is that all?"

"That's all." Ricki sighed. "I tried all different kinds of questions, like, 'How do you like the Shepherds' new house? Andy sure was working hard, huh? Vanessa sure has a nice dad, doesn't she?' But I heard no bells ringing or birds singing."

"Maybe not that you could notice," said Vanessa.

"Did you notice bells or birds around your dad?"

Vanessa shook her head. "Not really. But he did seem kind of . . . I don't know. Interested. I mean, he said your mom was nice, too. And that he's always felt glad I had found such nice people to be friends with. Then he

28

looked like he'd say more, but I couldn't think of a way to encourage him without making him suspicious.''

Ricki drummed her fingers on her chin. ''We've got to get them to see each other more. You know, more quality time. Not just when they pick us up from each other's houses and stuff.''

''But how? We can't set up a blind date.'' Vanessa frowned.

''Why not? Hey, great idea!'' Ricki sat up straight.

''It's a terrible idea. Talk about making them suspicious!''

''Oh.'' Ricki nestled back into the pillows. ''We need an excuse.''

''What do you mean?'' asked Vanessa.

''To get them together. I mean, some reason why they should spend, oh, a whole afternoon or something together,'' Ricki said.

''In a romantic setting,'' Vanessa added.

''Yeah. How about this? You tell your dad that my mom enjoys fixing old houses, and I tell Mom that your dad needs her help.''

''That's romantic?''

''I guess not. Too much hammering and sawing. Okay. Let's see. What's romantic?'' Ricki squinted, thinking.

''The ocean,'' Vanessa offered.

''Sure. We send them on an all-expenses-paid luxury cruise to Tahiti. Right. Dream on.''

''No, I mean our ocean,'' Vanessa explained. ''Here in California. It's only a half hour away.''

''Right,'' said Ricki. ''We inflate my Aunt Laura's rubber raft, spread out your Save the Dolphins beach towel in it, add a candle and some frozen pizza. . . .''

''Ricki, be serious.''

29

"I am serious. And practical. What else could we afford?"

"How about a picnic?" Vanessa suggested.

"A picnic." Ricki shrugged, then nodded. "On the beach. That does sound romantic. And practical."

"But how would we get them to the beach? With what excuse?"

"Us," Ricki said. "We'll be the excuse."

"You mean, we say we want to go, and they have to take us?" Vanessa asked. "But we've never asked both of them to take us anywhere. They always take turns driving."

"It's Single Parents' Day," announced Ricki.

"What is?"

"Whatever day we decide to go."

"But I've never heard of— Oh, I see," said Vanessa. "Single Parents' Day. 'Dad,' I'll say, 'Ricki and I realize how lucky we are to have found such great people to have as single parents, and . . .' "

Ricki took it up. " 'We know you're going to be a little shocked, Mom, but we'd like to celebrate a day in your honor.' "

"Will they fall for it?"

"Depends not on what we say but how we say it," answered Ricki. "Not too corny, you know?"

Vanessa nodded. "You're right. Like this: 'Dad, I have a great idea. I know it sounds corny, but . . .' "

"Uh-oh," Ricki interrupted. "I just thought of something. They both hate the outdoors."

"My father doesn't hate the outdoors." Vanessa gazed at her wildflowers poster. "He's just the type who enjoys looking at it from the car. Remember when he took us to Yosemite while my grandparents were visiting last year?"

"We stopped at scenic overlooks for pictures. In the car."

"Not one foot on a hiking trail, even though my grandfather brought his backpack, and my grandmother brought her canteen."

"Mom's the same way," Ricki admitted. "She likes thinking about the wilderness. But you know, the beach isn't exactly wilderness. Lots of people go to the beach, even in cars."

Vanessa nodded. "You're right. I think it would be fine."

"Okay. When?" asked Ricki.

"On a weekend, of course, when we're not in school."

"But not Saturday," Ricki said. "Mom works lots of Saturdays, and when she doesn't she's tired because it's the day after Friday."

"Oh, but on lots of Sundays Dad is tired because he plays Saturday night gigs until 2:00 A.M."

Ricki shook her head. "We don't want them to be tired. We want them to be friendly."

"And romantic."

"Okay, then. What should we do?" Ricki asked.

"Let's check their schedules," said Vanessa. "Tell them about Single Parents' Day, and ask them when they can celebrate it."

"By some miracle their schedules might cooperate. It seems hopeless." Ricki threw her hands in the air. "Are we nuts for trying this whole scheme, Vee? I mean, our parents are so different."

"Oh, come on, Ricki. We have to try. What harm can it do? The worst would be that we'd have a fun, cozy day together as if—"

"As if we were a family," Ricki said. "And the best that could happen is that they'd see how great it would be. How convenient. They wouldn't have to drive us back and forth to each other's houses anymore if we all lived together.''

Vanessa laughed. ''Right! It would be wonderful all around. And I thought of something. . . .''

''What?''

''Something else they have in common. The outdoors thing.''

''Yeah!'' agreed Ricki. ''Wow! There must be all kinds of similarities we just haven't thought of yet!''

Chapter 4

They couldn't have ordered a more beautiful day.

Vanessa sat next to Ricki in the backseat of Anita's small car enjoying the cool breeze. Finally, in the first week of October, fall seemed to be making an appearance. Anita drove on the freeway along San Francisco Bay, which reflected a clear blue sky.

"I'm freezing," Ricki whispered. "Would you shut your window?"

"Wear this." Vanessa pulled a jacket from the pile on the seat.

"I'm not a polar bear," Ricki replied, louder than she'd intended. She and Vanessa had agreed to be models of good behavior on Single Parents' Day. They had just finished French braiding each other's hair without one peep over how hard the comb pulled.

Vanessa sighed and rolled up her window.

"Vanessa is a polar bear, Ricki," Andy said. "Aren't you, Vee?" He turned around in the front seat to smile at his daughter. "Must be all that tough New England blood in her. Plus the fact that before we came to sunny California she spent her first six winters in Boston."

"Well, Ricki's a California girl all the way." Anita peeked at her in the rearview mirror. "She and I were both born out in the Central Valley, where it gets hot as blazes."

Andy faced forward again to talk with Anita. Vanessa looked at Ricki, who grinned back. Things were going just as they'd hoped. Both parents had agreed enthusiastically to the Single Parents' Day idea and had even switched their schedules around to free up a Sunday afternoon. Most important, they seemed to be getting along perfectly.

As they neared the coast, Vanessa read aloud road directions she had clipped from a newspaper article entitled "Wonderful Weekend Wanders." " 'Take Tennessee Valley Road straight to the parking lot. From there it's a short, lovely stroll to the beach.' "

"Sounds great," said Anita.

The parking lot was almost empty, which pleased her even more.

"The thing I hate about parks and whatnot," she told Andy as they all began gathering jackets and picnic supplies, "is crowds. I don't enjoy competing for a spot in the wide open spaces."

"Absolutely," Andy agreed. "It's a contradiction."

By the time they shut and locked the car doors, the four of them looked like a team of pack mules.

"Where'd all this stuff come from?" Ricki whispered to Vanessa.

"Food and drinks, paper plates, utensils and napkins, beach blankets and umbrella . . ." Vanessa listed.

"I just hope that the 'short, lovely stroll' is heavy on the 'short,' " Ricki said.

Andy led the way down the path. "Mmm, smells great out here."

"The ocean." Anita nodded from behind the enormous beach umbrella she carried. "It must not be far."

They walked single file. After a while Vanessa looked

at her watch. Fifteen minutes already. Could she have been reading about the wrong beach?

"Oh." Andy suddenly stopped dead in his tracks.

Anita piled right into his back. "Ah!"

"What?" asked Ricki, who managed to avoid running into her mother.

Vanessa, bringing up the rear, looked down at the side of the path where her father was pointing.

"Poison oak," he said.

"What?" said Anita, taking off her sunglasses. "That vine?"

Andy nodded.

Anita and the umbrella leaned over to look at it. "That's not poison oak."

"Really?" Andy peered at it. "Sure looks like poison oak."

"Not at all," Anita assured him. "Blackberry."

They continued walking.

Around every bend, Ricki expected to see the trail end on a sunny beach. But it kept going. She was just about to ask Vanessa if the newspaper had said anything about a long, winding trail bordered by what some people may fear is poison oak, when something whacked her in the face. Before she could peel the something away from her eyes, a gust of wind did it for her.

"My hat!" her mother wailed.

Ricki whirled to see her mom's straw boater whiz away like a Frisbee.

"I'll get it." Andy dashed past them down the trail.

"Oh, my," Vanessa said, breathing a sigh.

Her father looked a little like a kitten chasing a butterfly. He ran and jumped, ran and jumped, trying to catch the hat that glided on a draft just inches out of his grasp.

Anita ran after him.

"I told her that was a goofy hat to wear," Ricki yelled to Vanessa above the rising wind.

Andy suddenly took a mighty leap and nabbed the runaway hat. The girls clapped. But just as quickly, he dropped it into the gully, where it caught on a vine.

He and Anita stood staring at it. The wind whipped at Andy's longish hair and plastered Anita's yellow skirt against her legs.

"Where did this wind come from?" Ricki wondered aloud. She could see Andy and Anita talking but couldn't hear them. "And what are they waiting for?"

"He's horribly allergic to poison oak," said Vanessa.

"Mom says it's blackberry," Ricki said.

"Then why doesn't she go down and get her hat?" asked Vanessa.

"She hates it when someone doesn't take her word for something. She's probably trying to convince him it's blackberry, just on principle."

"Oh, my," sighed Vanessa. She held onto her green sun visor.

Finally, Anita stepped into the bramble and retrieved her hat.

Andy pointed at it as they approached the girls. "Is it okay?"

Anita picked leaves off the brim. "Fine. Thanks."

"Don't mention it."

"Let's press on, girls," Anita said, taking the lead.

Ricki bit her lip. She knew that tone in her mother's voice. Too polite.

The wind kept up, blowing wisps of fog through the little valley. They trudged on. Vanessa began to wonder if a picnic at the kitchen table wouldn't have been more romantic. But just then Ricki cried, "The beach!"

Ahead lay a beautiful stretch of blue—the ocean. And

miraculously, the wind began to die. By the time the four of them stepped off the path onto golden sand, the day had turned calm and sunny again.

Vanessa swallowed in relief. Single Parents' Day had to go well.

She and Ricki got busy setting up the umbrella, spreading out the blankets, and arranging the sacks and thermoses. Their parents admired the view. They even started chatting again.

Ricki grinned. Vanessa grinned back.

"Vee, what are those birds out there on the rocks?" her father asked. "Ducks?"

From her backpack, Vanessa pulled her compact field glasses, a Christmas present from her grandparents.

"They're gulls, Dad. Western gulls. And a couple of brown pelicans. Want to see?"

They passed the field glasses around.

"Hey, seals!" Ricki cried. "On those rocks out there."

"Actually," said Vanessa, "they're California sea lions, which are bigger than the local harbor seals and have external ears."

"Details, details." Ricki rolled her eyes.

"I'm always impressed by your knowledge about the natural world, Vanessa." Anita put her hat back on, tucking her short black curls under it. "I think it's becoming more than a hobby for you, isn't it? You might wind up as a biologist or naturalist."

Vanessa gave a little shrug. "I'd like that. But mostly I just read about things."

"And when we took a class field trip to the Marine Mammal Center, you memorized everything," Ricki said.

Andy tugged at the green ribbon in Vanessa's braid. "Any sharks around here?"

Vanessa nodded. "Great whites. They eat seals and sea lions."

"Great white sharks? Here?" Anita's eyes went wide.

"Maybe not today," said Vanessa. "But they have been sighted."

Ricki poked Vanessa in the ribs. "Don't worry, Mom. We're not swimming." She whispered to Vanessa, "Sharks aren't romantic."

"Oh, um, sightings are very rare," said Vanessa. "Attacks on humans are extremely rare. They prefer gobbling up marine mammals."

Ricki poked her again and whispered, "Don't say that!"

"All this talk of gobbling." Andy spread out on the blanket and leaned on an elbow. "What's for lunch?"

To Ricki's surprise, her mother laughed. Mom didn't have a strong stomach for talk about gory stuff. Even more surprising, her mother settled down next to Andy, folding her long legs under her skirt.

"How about our special homemade fruit punch for starters?" Vanessa suggested.

They poured cups full of punch and passed them around, then brought out the container of guacamole dip and a bag of taco chips.

"Mmm," said Anita. "Excellent dip. Just like Uncle Mario's."

Ricki smiled guiltily. "That's 'cause it *is* Uncle Mario's."

"Ricki asked him for the recipe because we knew you both really like it," Vanessa explained, "and he said he had made too much this week anyway and had one of his delivery guys drop it off."

Anita shook her head. "My brother feels it's his mission in life to fill the world with Mexican food."

"Fine by me," said Andy. "This is good stuff."

"Glad you like it," said Ricki, "because he also gave us these." She pulled four foil-wrapped burritos out of the paper sack.

"Poor girls." Andy laughed. "Slaving over a hot stove for us."

Vanessa lifted her chin. "Wait. We're not through."

Ricki brought out the big salad the two of them had made Friday afternoon. Then for dessert there were fudge brownies that Vanessa had baked, while Ricki helped by tasting the batter.

"Delicious," said Anita when they finished. "Thank you." She smiled at them over the tops of her sunglasses.

Andy nodded. "Single Parents' Day should come more often."

Vanessa and Ricki sneaked glances at each other and tried not to beam too brightly. Things were working out!

They gathered up the remains of lunch, then joined their parents in the shade of the umbrella, staring out to sea and dozing.

Vanessa scanned the distant waves with her field glasses.

"Anything out there?" asked Anita.

"Could be humpback whales this time of year," Vanessa said. "California gray whales haven't begun their migration quite yet."

"It's amazing they've got a migration at all," said Andy. He was lying on the blanket, one arm flung over his eyes. "Weren't they nearly extinct not long ago?"

Vanessa nodded. "By the turn of the century there were only a few thousand left, because whalers killed so many. But then laws were passed to protect them."

"That's wonderful." Anita sighed.

"This whole coast should be a marine sanctuary," said Andy. "Everything should be protected."

"We do have a magnificent resource here," Anita agreed. "So beautiful. But a sanctuary wouldn't be practical right now."

"Why not?" Andy pulled his arm away from his eyes.

"Too much industry depends on our ocean and bays." Anita gazed out at the crashing surf.

Ricki watched the surf, too, because it was gradually turning from clear green to murky brown as a bank of fog moved in overhead.

"Industry needs to change," said Andy. "We can't keep wearing out nature. We overfish, spill oil, dump all kinds of junk—"

"Jobs depend on the system as it is now," interrupted Anita. "You can't change things overnight. Thousands of people would be put out of work."

"Clean air and water don't have to put people out of work," Andy shot back. "You're using an old excuse, Anita."

"You're not being realistic, Andy. You work in your home, by yourself. You're not out in the world like I am."

"Oh-ho! So I'm just a guitar picker, and you're a woman of the world? Come on, Anita, you—"

"It's raining," Vanessa said.

Everyone looked up. The ocean's surface was spattered by raindrops. A steady thumping began on the umbrella, on the paper sacks and backpacks, and any parts of the blankets that weren't covered. In seconds, it seemed, the sky had gone from brilliant blue to dark, threatening gray.

"We should go," Anita said.

Ricki moved further under the umbrella. "Maybe it will

pass, Mom. This could be just one of those squalls or something.''

Andy pointed at the sky. "I think your mother is right. We seem to be in for some weather.''

Vanessa's heart sank. They couldn't leave now, on such a sour note, in the middle of an argument and a rainstorm. That wouldn't be romantic at all!

"It never rains in October," she protested. "This is a fluke.''

"Come on, girls. Let's get going.'' Anita was obviously not going to change her mind.

While gathering their belongings, they all got soaked. By the time they reached the trail leading back to the car, they were dripping. And very quickly the trail itself turned into something much more like a creek. Water and mud everywhere.

Back at the car they tossed everything into the trunk, then hurried to open the doors and jump in.

"Your upholstery . . .'' said Andy.

"Doesn't matter,'' Anita answered.

And those were the only words the two of them spoke to each other for most of the ride home.

Chapter 5

Under her desk Vanessa held the note Ricki had passed her. She quickly unfolded it. WE HAVE TO TALK ABOUT YESTERDAY, it read.

She nodded at Ricki, keeping an eye on their teacher, Mr. Sambucchio. Not that he was good at catching note passers. In fact, Mr. Sambucchio wasn't good at catching many classroom crimes. But better safe than sorry.

"Ms. Thompsen, on which continent is the nation of Mexico?" Mr. Sambucchio quietly asked a red-haired girl named Sally. A tall man with pale skin, big ears, a thin black mustache, and gangly arms and legs, he did everything quietly.

"Um, North America?" Sally answered.

"Very good, yes. North America is our own continent, as well." Mr. Sambucchio straightened his yellow bow tie. "Ms. Romero? Brazil is on which continent?"

Ricki looked up at him in surprise. Vanessa could see that she had been busy writing another note. She held her breath. Back in the fourth grade, she and Ricki got in trouble constantly for passing notes. Before that, in third grade, one of the ways they became friends was by getting in trouble together for having a giggling fit in the middle of penmanship class. Vanessa hated getting in trouble.

But Ricki wasn't worried. Thoughtfully, she tapped a

finger on her chin. "I'm not sure I know the answer to that question, Mr. Sambucchio. Do you have another one?"

Mr. Sambucchio cleared his throat and smoothed back hairs on his balding crown. "No, at the moment I don't. Please study geography more thoroughly for tomorrow. Brazil is in South America."

Ricki gave Vanessa a quick grin.

Oh, Ricki, Vanessa said to herself, only half-grinning back.

At the lunch table Louise Ann Robbins set her tray down next to them and shook her head at Ricki. "You are just too cool. Poor teacher doesn't stand a chance."

"Mr. Sam's a nice guy. I don't have it in for him." Ricki shrugged.

Dani de Avila, the new girl from the Philippines, said, "Yes, I think the teacher is very nice. He's very pah-tient."

"Pay-tient," Louise Ann corrected.

"Pay-tient." Dani smiled at Louise Ann, her new best friend.

Louise Ann smiled back. Along with Vanessa, she was one of the smartest people in sixth grade. She was also one of the cutest girls, with big dark eyes and smooth dark skin.

"I—I like your bracelet, Louise Ann," said Kimberly Morris through a mouthful of mashed potatoes. Her dish-water blond hair hung in a pageboy around her bright pink cheeks. The shyest girl in sixth grade, Kimberly always sat close to Vanessa.

"Oh, you do? Thanks. It's from Africa. My mom calls it an *urafiki* bracelet. That's supposed to mean friendship in Swahili." She slipped the bangle of red and green bead-work off her wrist for Kimberly to see. She got to wear

43

all kinds of unusual things because her mother and aunts owned an African imports boutique in San Francisco.

"In Tagalog, the language of my country, friendship is *kaibigan*." Dani's pretty brown eyes turned in a smile to each of the four girls.

Ricki added, "I think it's *amistad* in Spanish. My family is Mexican-American, but I only speak Spanish to my grandparents."

"*Urafiki, kaibigan, amistad,* friendship," Vanessa recited. She liked the sound of the words. And she liked the little group that she and Ricki had been having lunch with that year. It was nice to talk to the same girls every day instead of having to get to know different people. She wasn't at all like Ricki, who easily made friends with anyone she wanted.

"Oh, for heavens sake," said Louise Ann.

Ricki followed her stare to the lunch line.

"Courtney's going to do it again," Louise Ann said.

Right on cue, the cafeteria filled with loud shouts. Courtney Haines's shouts. Kids standing in the lunch line cleared a big space for Courtney to do her sideways splits football cheer.

Ricki groaned. "I feel sick. That's the third time today."

"Is it the mashed potatoes?" asked Kimberly, pushing at her big blue-framed glasses. "Mine don't taste good, either."

They all turned to look at her. Kimberly did fine in school but never seemed to know what was going on around her.

"Courtney told a bunch of people last week that she wants everybody to think of her as cheerleading material," said Louise Ann. "There'll be a squad next year, in junior high."

Ricki rolled her eyes. "Cheerleading is dumb. Super dumb."

"Well, are you kids having a good time?"

Ricki looked up to find Courtney, flanked by her friends Paige Wallis and Heather Hurst, smiling down on them like Miss Congeniality.

Everyone fell silent. Courtney not only acted older than most sixth-graders, but she looked older, too. You could sometimes see the outline of a real bra through her blouse. The boys made jokes about it. And her mother let her wear high heels and lots of makeup.

Most of the girls felt kind of in awe of her. Ricki did, too, sometimes, but not for long.

"Sure," Ricki answered. "Having fun with those *great* cheers?"

Vanessa cringed. Ricki could make the most innocent words sound sarcastic.

Courtney pushed at a puff of her moussed-up, honey brown hair. "Mmm-hmm. Well, we'll see you *kids* later."

"She's very beautiful," whispered Dani after Courtney left. "I would like to be so beautiful, to have the boys stare at me."

"I'm going to be sick again. Are you boy crazy?" asked Ricki.

"Boy crazy?" Dani looked puzzled.

"It's when all you think about is boys," Vanessa explained.

"I like boys," said Dani. "I have a boyfriend."

Kimberly widened her gray-blue eyes. "You do?"

Dani's shiny cap of black hair bobbed in a nod. "Rafael. In Manila, the city where I'm from. He writes to me."

"There must be better choices there," Louise Ann said.

45

"I sure wouldn't want any of the clowns around here for a boyfriend."

"Me, neither," Ricki agreed. "Never in a million years."

"Some of them are nice, maybe just as friends," said Vanessa.

"Ben's our friend, isn't he?" Kimberly asked. "He's nice."

"Schuyler Simmons seems to think he's our friend, always hanging around," said Ricki. "But he's sure not anyone's boyfriend."

"Ugh," Louise Ann grunted. "Never. He's such a pest."

"That is Schuyler?" Dani pointed at a short, skinny boy with greasy, mouse brown hair a few tables away.

Ricki grabbed Dani's pointing finger and lowered it. "Yes, that's Schuyler, but don't get his attention."

"Which one is Ben?" Dani asked.

"In the blue shirt, by the drinking fountain," Vanessa said.

"Oh! He's very handsome!" Dani cried.

"Yeah." Ricki grinned. "And he's in love with Vanessa."

Vanessa rolled her eyes. "No, he's not."

"Sure he is. Has been since third grade."

Kimberly's eyes went wide again.

Louise Ann explained, "He had a crush on Vanessa and sent her love notes every day."

Vanessa blushed. "That was in third grade."

"Love never dies." Ricki put her hands over her heart. Then she saw the look on her friend's face and shut up fast. Vanessa's lips pressed together tightly, and her delicate little chin jutted out.

Ricki felt like kicking herself. Vanessa never could take

much teasing. She got embarrassed really easily. The bell rang just as Ricki was trying to think of a way to change the subject.

On the way back to class, Ricki took Vanessa aside. "You mad?"

"No-o-o." Vanessa drew the word out in an impatient way.

"You look mad."

"You just act so childish sometimes." Vanessa crossed her arms.

"Well, you're too touchy," Ricki tossed back. "I was only joking."

"It's rude to make jokes like that."

"Oh, Vee, just stand up for yourself. If you don't like somebody teasing you, talk back!"

Vanessa let out a sigh. "I'm not quick like you, Ricki. It's hard to think of things to say right away."

Ricki bunched her mouth to the side. "Sorry. I didn't mean to hurt your feelings at the lunch table."

"You didn't really." Vanessa smiled weakly. "I was just . . . embarrassed."

"Well, okay. You know what? We're going to be late."

"I know," Vanessa said. "And we haven't even talked about the picnic. How about when you come home with me tomorrow afternoon?"

Ricki nodded. The two of them dashed down the hall and slipped under Mr. Sambucchio's arm just as he was shutting the door.

"Ee-uu! Yuck!" Ricki held a strip of the ugliest wall-paper she had ever seen. She, Andy, and Vanessa were in the kitchen of the Mariposa Lane house. "Why would anyone have gone to the trouble of putting this up?"

"For the same reason," Andy replied, "that we're taking it down. Personal taste. Avocado green used to be a very popular color."

"With this brown-and-pink flower print on it? You're kidding."

"It's hideous," Vanessa agreed.

Andy laughed. "Hmm. Maybe we should leave it up, just for entertainment's sake."

"No!" Both girls groaned at once.

The three of them kept stripping the paper off the wall.

After a couple of minutes, Vanessa glanced at Ricki and silently mouthed the question, "Now?"

Ricki nodded. They had hatched a plan back at the duplex, before Andy convinced them to help him at the new house. For Ricki, it hadn't taken much convincing. She enjoyed all the banging and tearing down. It was kind of like a demolition derby. But in recent weeks Vanessa had already hammered her thumb twice, gotten splinters in her knees and paint in her hair. Home improvement was not her favorite way to spend an afternoon. Still, for the sake of the Sisters Scheme, she had gone along. And now it was time.

"Um, we had an interesting assignment in social studies last week," Vanessa said.

"Really?" Andy was busy scraping at a stubborn spot.

Vanessa nodded. "We were supposed to look in the newspaper for articles about different candidates in the utilities board race and see how their opinions differed."

"Mmm," said Andy.

Ricki cleared his throat. "Politics is very interesting. Don't you think so?"

"Me?" Andy glanced at her. "Sure. Sometimes I volunteer on campaigns, stuffing envelopes or whatever. I haven't followed the utilities board race, though."

"Yeah, neither has my mom," said Ricki. "But she's

48

interested in politics, too. She likes talking about stuff like that.''

Andy kept scraping wallpaper.

''She enjoys having political discussions with people, even if sometimes they end up arguing.'' Ricki glanced at Vanessa, who was chewing worriedly on the inside of her cheek. Maybe she wasn't being subtle enough. Every word she had said was true but maybe just laid on too thick.

Andy rested the scraper on his knee. ''Is that right?''

Ricki nodded, taking a deep breath.

As Andy turned back to the wallpaper, the girls noticed that he hid a very small grin under his beard.

The Scheme forged full steam ahead.

Friday afternoon after Ricki's soccer practice at school, Anita took the girls to the mall for pizza and shopping.

''These feel great,'' Ricki said while trying on a pair of neon orange running shoes. ''But they're too tight.''

''How can shoes feel great if they're too tight?'' her mother wanted to know.

Ricki shrugged. ''They just do.''

''I think you just like the way they look.''

''They're cool.'' Ricki admired the lime green racing stripes in the store mirror. ''Maybe they'll stretch.''

''Shoes never stretch.'' Vanessa shook her head. ''Not really.''

''You're absolutely right, hon.'' Anita nodded, then whispered, ''Stretchability is a myth concocted by shoe salesmen long ago. It survives to this day in spite of blisters and calluses and bunions.''

Ricki finally found a pair that felt good, looked reasonably cool, and didn't cause her mother to have a fit at the cash register.

On their way out of the mall, she reached behind her

mother and tapped Vanessa's shoulder. "Now?" she mouthed. They had been waiting for the right moment all evening. Vanessa nodded.

"We had an interesting assignment in social studies last week," Ricki began.

The conversation took off from there, going much as it had with Vanessa's father. In the car, Anita was busy dodging parking lot traffic and didn't pay much attention until Vanessa said, "Dad enjoys political discussions, even if sometimes they end up in arguments."

Anita stopped at a light and turned to look at Vanessa on the passenger side. "He does?"

"Mmm-hmm." Vanessa glanced at Ricky for encouragement.

Horns brayed from the line of cars behind them. Anita stared straight at the stoplight but didn't notice that it had turned green. She didn't move, in fact, until Ricki said, "Mom, the light."

"Oh!" Anita started the car forward.

Vanessa raised her eyebrows at Ricki, who winked back.

Chapter 6

"There's something between them. I just know there is." Vanessa sat cross-legged on Ricki's bed, browsing through the Saturday paper.

Ricki nodded. "The question is, what? Are our parents in love with each other, or do they hate each other's guts?"

"Do you really think they might hate each other?" Vanessa asked.

She watched Ricki make faces at herself in the mirror over her dresser. Ricki had been doing that a lot since Thursday, when Ms. Abbott in art class told her she had "expressive, elastic features."

Ricki shut one eye, arched the opposite eyebrow, and bared her teeth. "No. I think our parents are in love. But it's hard to prove, considering how they act around each other."

"Their horrible fight at the picnic," Vanessa said.

"Not only that, but every time they've seen each other in the two weeks since then they've acted so normal. I mean, just as if nothing happened. As if they couldn't care less about each other." Ricki opened her mouth wide and stuck out her tongue.

"But when I mention your mother," said Vanessa, blond eyebrows knit in a frown, "even just that she's

51

coming to pick me up or something, Dad gets really weird. Like your mother acted at that stoplight.''

Ricki nodded. "Listen to this. When I mention your dad around Mom, she starts dropping things.''

"Really?"

"In the kitchen last week, I told her about your dad's new music compositions, and she dropped a whole frozen cherry pie. She said it was slippery because of the moisture from the freezer.''

Vanessa smiled gleefully. "This is wonderful!''

"I guess so.'' Ricki tried to wiggle an ear. "But what good is it going to do if all our parents ever do is stare off into space and drop things? We'll never become sisters.''

"They need to see each other more often. More romantically.''

"Hey, don't forget how our last try at that worked out.''

"How could I?'' Vanessa asked. "The romantic picnic by the sea. Doesn't it seem like every time they get together it ends in disaster? I mean, remember the time a couple of years ago, when your mom and my dad helped drive our class to The Exploratorium museum in San Francisco?''

Ricki nodded. "There was an earthquake.''

Vanessa sighed. "Do you think they'll get into more arguments about politics or whatever?''

Ricki grabbed a handful of hair and piled it on top of her head. She turned back and forth to check out her profiles. "Your guess is as good as mine. They're just so darn different. Hey, how would I look with short hair?''

Vanessa continued leafing through the paper. "You can't cut it unless I do.''

"Why not?"

"Because we agreed.''

"So you cut yours, too.'' Ricki let her hair fall back

down to her shoulders, then fluffed out her bangs with her fingers. "Well, aren't you going to argue with me?"

"Be quiet a minute."

"Why?" Ricki glanced at Vanessa, who was busy reading.

"Just hush."

Ricki flopped down next to Vanessa on the bed.

"Oh, my," Vanessa said.

"You're always saying that. Oh, your *what?*"

"Hush."

Ricki rolled her eyes. A minute later Vanessa held an article in her face.

Ricki read the headline. " 'Love Guide for the Year 2000.' So?"

" 'Love and romance are not what they used to be,' " Vanessa read. " 'Do the personal ads work? Should women ask men out? Do opposites attract? These are old questions, to which Deborah Mindenthal's new book, *Love Guide to the New Century,* gives new answers.' "

"Wow! 'Do opposites attract?' That's just what we need to know!" Ricki exclaimed.

"Exactly," said Vanessa. "We need to read that book."

"But we can't afford to buy it. I've cut back photography to just one roll a week, and Mom is still complaining."

"Still? But she said you could buy one roll."

"I guess I got some other stuff, too. Lens-cleaning paper, a photo album . . . She'll flip if I spend more."

"Well, we don't have to spend a penny, Ricki. Haven't you ever heard of the library?"

"Oh, yeah. I'll call Mom at work. She said not to leave the house while she was gone, but I'm sure she'll let us walk to the branch library. It's only two blocks away.

She'll probably keel over, though, when she hears I want to spend Saturday afternoon there!''

A half hour later they stood at the library information desk.

"I'll ask where the love guides are," Ricki said.

Vanessa grabbed her arm. "No! How embarrassing!''

"I guess you're going to insist on the card catalog again." Ricki sighed. Vanessa never took the easy way.

"What is wrong with using the card catalog?" Vanessa turned up her nose and marched to the reference tables. "It's even on computer. Oh, Ricki! Look!''

"What?''

"This." Vanessa pointed to a stack of flyers pinned on a notice board. " 'Community center photography class. Learn to process your own film.' Where's the community center?''

"Right next door. That yellow building.''

"Then it's perfect. If you learn to process your own film, you won't have to pay the camera shop to do it, right?''

Ricki read the notice. "Wow, Vee. That's a great idea." She took one of the flyers and studied it while Vanessa looked for the *Love Guide* in the library computer.

Within minutes the two of them had settled at a secluded corner table behind a potted palm.

" 'Chapter One,' " Ricki whispered. " 'New Choices.' ''

"Wait. Let's skim through," whispered Vanessa. "The table of contents says there's a section on opposites attracting. Ah, here it is.''

" 'To some, it's an old wives' tale,' " Ricki read. " 'To others, it's a reliable key to matchmaking. Experts agree that there is something to the notion of divergent personalities appealing to one another.' What's divergent?''

"Different," Vanessa answered, then read on. " 'Sparks often fly from friction, whether it is between two sticks or two people. Dramatic differences between individuals can create excitement—even tempestuous romance.' ''

"Tempestuous?" asked Ricki.

"It means stormy," Vanessa said.

"Well, we sure had that at the picnic, didn't we?"

Vanessa ignored her. "Isn't this wonderful? Our parents' differences—even their arguments—could lead them to romance!''

Ricki took up the reading. " 'Psychologists explain that partners in almost every relationship, including friendship, look to one another for qualities they themselves lack. A shy person may enjoy an outgoing companion. Or a talkative person may appreciate someone more quiet. Of course, not all relationships are built on differences. And problems may arise if partners are too different.' Uh-oh, what if our parents are too different, Vee?''

"Well, look. It says, 'Members of a relationship must share basic values, regardless of how their personal styles vary.' ''

Ricki tapped a finger on her chin. "Basic values? Do they mean, like, morals? What's right, and what's wrong?''

"I think so," Vanessa said. "How people feel deep down in their hearts about things.''

"Your dad and my mom are both nice. I mean, underneath it all.''

Vanessa nodded. "I think they share values. You and I are best friends, and we're their children. That must mean something.''

"Good point!" Ricki agreed. "Yeah!" She shut the book with a thud. "We don't have to worry. They're made for each other."

Vanessa smiled. "Do you really think so?"

"It's going to happen, Vee. I can feel it in my bones."

"You know, Ricki, I think I can, too. I mean, I don't know how to explain it, but . . ."

"It seems right, doesn't it? Heck, *we* should have written this book." Ricki jumped up and put the *Love Guide* on the shelf.

Vanessa took the book down and set it on the table. "Ricki, you're not supposed to reshelve library books."

"Details, Vee," Ricki said, "details. We have more important things to discuss—a new plan."

Ricki watched her mother read the flyer about the photography class. "Well? Doesn't this sound great, Mom? Huh?"

Her mother sat in her big white side chair under a black metal reading lamp. The living room looked a lot like the kitchen—mostly black and white. Ricki knelt on the chair's ottoman.

"Stop," her mom said.

"Stop what?"

"Bouncing up and down. You'll ruin the springs."

"I'm excited," Ricki explained.

"I can see that. But this class meets Thursday evenings, honey. I may not always get home in time to take you, and you can't walk."

"It's only two blocks!"

"It's at night, and you'll be alone. Forget it."

Ricki bounced again. She couldn't help it. "Mo-om!"

"Please don't whine. This class just won't work."

"You yell at me for spending too much on my pictures—"

"I don't 'yell.' I tell you the way things are."

"I'm trying to do something about it. This class would save money." Ricki tried very hard not to whine and got off the ottoman so she wouldn't bounce.

Her mother took off her red-framed reading glasses. "We'll have to try something else, hon. There might be photography classes in the junior high next year. I've heard that school has excellent facilities."

"Next year! Mom, that's *next year*. What about now?"

"Sometimes we have to be patient."

Ricki sighed and dropped onto the white sofa. Patience, she thought. One of her mom's favorite words. Sometimes she thought she might scream if she heard it one more time.

"You have hobbies, Mom. *You* don't have to wait till next year. You became a member of that racquetball club."

"I call that exercise, not a hobby," her mother said. "I really don't have much time for hobbies."

"I know, because you have to work so hard to put food on the table and a roof over our heads and—"

"Ricki, are you getting sarcastic with me?"

Ricki picked at a scab on her knuckle. "I just mean, I—"

"Honey, I know. You deserve to explore your interests. I support that one hundred percent. The photography class is a very good idea. Maybe there's one on a different day."

Ricki frowned, then shrugged. "There might be. I could call the community center."

"Good. They can probably make suggestions. Meanwhile, hon, do you think of me as a tight-fisted ogre?"

Ricki couldn't help smiling. "Sometimes."

"Well, we really do have to stay on our budget," her mom said. "But I also want you to have the things you need, including a good education. And I think your interest in photography is part of that."

"You do?"

"Of course. Now come over here."

Ricki squeezed into the chair next to her mother for a big hug.

"Mom?" she said after a while. "Don't forget that Vee's spending the night Friday. I told her we could make pizza."

"Oh, that's right. Okay. I'll get the dough mix tomorrow."

"Her dad will bring her over."

"Andy?"

"Yup, that's his name." Ricki wiggled forward so that she could see her mother's face. That was part of the new Sisters Scheme—to watch the reactions of each parent to the other.

To her disappointment there was no reaction. No signs of tempestuous romance, or even thoughts about it. Oh, well, Ricki told herself. Mom must be trying to act cool.

Vanessa dipped her brush into a bucket of the cream-colored paint she and her father had chosen for the kitchen walls. "Dad?"

"Hmm?" He was busy attacking the ceiling with a long-handled roller brush.

"Don't forget, I'm spending tomorrow night at Ricki's." Vanessa climbed one rung higher on the stepladder to reach a corner.

"Oh, I had fogotten." Andy wiped a spatter of paint off his elbow onto his jeans. "In fact, I was thinking we'd make that flounder florentine you like for dinner."

"I'm having pizza at Ricki's."

"So I figured," said her father. "You always have pizza at Ricki's. I think *they* always have pizza."

"Anita gets this special mix for the dough. It's yummy. Don't forget, you said you'd take me over about six o'clock."

Andy turned back to his roller brushing. "I remember."

Vanessa frowned. She wasn't getting much of a reaction at all out of her father these days, when it came to Anita. But that didn't matter, she decided. The important part would come with the "special encounters" she and Ricki planned. Really, the encounters weren't so special—just the ordinary, every day, one-parent-drops-kid-off-at-the-other's-house type of thing, plus whatever other chance meetings she and Ricki could set up. The idea was to keep trying to get their parents together, then let true love take its course.

She looked at her watch. "Dad, it's four-thirty. I'm sick of painting. Anyway, it's my practice time."

He nodded. "Your cello's in the living room, isn't it?"

"Yes," Vanessa said. She wanted to add, if you can call it a living room, but buttoned her lip. That month she had been trying to cooperate and not be so negative about the house, as Ricki and her father had both asked her to do. But she still felt uncomfortable there, with everything out of order, so haphazard and temporary.

The kitchen, she had to admit, looked much better than it used to. But the new cabinets hadn't come yet, or the sink, and there were no appliances except for a knee-high refrigerator that her dad's artist friend Maureen had lent him. Finally, Andy had admitted that they couldn't move in by Christmas. Now he was talking about April.

In the living room, Vanessa found her cello among stacked-up paint cans and lumber. At least that was an improvement over what used to be there—old mattresses and trash from earlier tenants.

Out on the porch, Vanessa settled into a chair. After tuning the strings with the pegs on her cello's neck, she started with a series of music exercises to strengthen her fingers. Her cello teacher was a real stickler about finger excercises.

Later, in the middle of a piece by Mozart, she thought of her mother. The melody reminded her of one her mama used to sing to her. The cello itself sometimes sounded like her mother's clear, beautiful voice. Celeste used to sing all kinds of songs to her at bedtime—opera, folk songs, tunes she'd make up. Nowadays, bedtime was when Vanessa usually thought of her mother. Unless, of course, she got a letter from her, which only happened about every two months.

"Nice, Vee, very nice." Her father's words came from behind the screen door after she finished the sonata. He walked out to the porch. "Especially your phrasing. Very expressive."

"Thanks." Vanessa smiled, taking a little bow.

"Ready to go home soon? It's close to six."

Vanessa nodded. "Sure."

Andy lowered himself into one of the plastic chairs. He propped his feet up on the railing, gazing out over the front yard. "You're still not enthusiastic about living here, are you, Vee?"

"I stopped complaining. Do I have to act excited, too?"

"Not act." Andy pulled his feet from the railing and set them back on the wooden porch floor. "I don't mean to hound you. It's just that I'm concerned. I'd hoped that once things started to shape up around here, you might begin to like it better."

"It is better," Vanessa admitted.

"Then why do you still seem . . . anxious?"

Vanessa shrugged. "The house is still pretty much a mess. I mean, it's getting better, but, . . . I don't know. There are other things, too. . . ."

"Like?"

"Well, like why didn't you ever ask me if I wanted to live here before you bought it? It's too late now. And it seems you told the whole world about it, except me." Her words came out in a flood that she'd been holding back for weeks.

Andy looked straight at Vanessa, then sighed. "I was wrong on that. I guess I . . . Well, for one thing I had to act really fast to buy this house. And for another, Vee, you are the most important person in the world to me. The last thing I wanted was for you to feel left out. But I've always promised you that someday we'd have a home of our own, and I knew how badly you wanted pets, so . . . I guess I wanted to surprise you."

"Surprise me?" Vanessa found herself grinning. She managed not to say: Surprise me with *this* place? Sometimes it was hard to decide whether her father was the sweetest man in the world or the most goofy.

She sighed. "I'm confused. Ricki really likes this house. She says it'll be great, and I guess she's right, but . . ."

"The change is scary," Andy provided. "Moving away from Mrs. Quan's, right?"

Vanessa's eyes started to fill. "I feel like such a baby."

Andy got up and squatted beside her chair. "Rainbow," he whispered, smoothing a lock of hair out of her eyes. "We had some difficult times a few years ago, during the divorce. Change can be hard, I know. But sometimes

61

change is for the better. I want this house to be a good change for us, and I really think it will.''

He smiled, and the love in his soft brown eyes made Vanessa feel about two hundred percent better.

Chapter 7

Courtney Haines, head of the student committee for the Halloween carnival, strutted around the classroom collecting posters people had volunteered to make.

"Where are yours, Ricki?" Vanessa whispered across the aisle.

Ricki shrugged. "I forgot all about it."

"Ricki, you're kidding! Ms. Abbott is counting on these. The carnival is only a week away!"

"Got too busy," Ricki said. "Can I borrow one of yours?"

"You always do this," Vanessa said.

"Do what?"

"Quiet, please," Mr. Sambucchio said. His commands always sounded more like requests.

Vanessa plunked down one of her posters on Ricki's desk.

In just seconds, Courtney sauntered up. "This is interesting, Ricki. Yours looks a lot like Vanessa's."

Ricki stuck her tongue out at Courtney's back when she flounced away. Vanessa sighed.

Later, at recess, she and Ricki played four square with Louise Ann, Kimberly, and Dani until Mr. Sambucchio came along practically dragging Ben Kumar and a red-haired boy named Randall Mott.

"These young men would like to share your game," said Mr. Sambucchio.

Recently the teachers had decided that the boys and the girls should play together at recess, instead of separating into different groups. So far, none of the kids went out of their way to cooperate.

Ricki was used to playing sports with boys on her soccer and softball teams. It wasn't too awful. Kimberly, though, almost froze in shyness when Ben and Randall joined their group. Vanessa got nervous, too. And Dani turned into a pile of giggles. Only Louise Ann took it in stride.

"Here," Louise Ann said, bouncing the ball to Ben.

Randall waited in line behind Ricki and Dani for a turn in the square.

"Way to go, Benny-Boy," Ricki called when he bounced Louise Ann out. She gave Vanessa a quick glance. Poor Vee still felt shy around Ben because of those old love notes, even though he seemed to have forgotten all about them.

Ben's brown eyes grinned at Ricki from under a shock of brown hair. "Thanks, *Mickey*."

Dani giggled. "What funny names you give to each other."

"Is your name short for something?" Randall asked her.

"Oh, yes. My full name is Daniela Raquel Jimenez de Avila."

Louise Ann gasped. "Whew, that's impressive!"

"Hey, did you say your middle name is Raquel?" Ricki asked. "That's my name, too. One of my aunts came up with Ricki for short."

"Hmm," Ben said. "That's what we'll call you. Raquel. You give everyone else nicknames. Yours will be a nickname in reverse."

Ricki shrugged. "I couldn't care less."

"What couldn't you care less about?" The voice came from behind Ricki. She turned to find Schuyler, hands in pockets, with that usual snide grin on his pale, thin face.

"She doesn't care what we call her," said Randall.

Ricki bounced the ball to Vanessa. "Keep your mouth shut, Schuyler. Don't try to be witty, because you never are."

Vanessa passed the ball on to Kimberly, thinking all the while how cool Ricki was. Her words to Schuyler didn't sound mean—just firm. In turn, Schuyler always obeyed her, never daring to make any of his cutting remarks to her or to Vanessa, her best friend. But he did pick on others—plenty.

"Well, Kimbo-Bimbo cares, doesn't she?" he said to Kimberly.

Kimberly blushed. Vanessa knew how she hated being teased.

"Kimbo-Bimbo," Schuyler repeated. "The brain."

Vanessa wished Kimberly would say something sharp back. But she just mumbled, "I'm not a bimbo!"

That spurred Schuyler on. "The Brain of Kennedy School!"

Ricki listened to the conversation with only mild interest. She was thinking about the soccer game coming up next week.

Why didn't Ricki do something? Vanessa wondered. She was the only one who could stop Schuyler.

Ricki caught a kind of pleading look from Vanessa.

"Oh," she finally mouthed. Then she sighed, and almost off-handedly said to Schuyler over her shoulder, "You're being a pain."

"Oh, yeah?" Schuyler said.

"Yeah. Bug off."

"Bzzz," he hummed, flapping his arms like wings. "Bzzz."

Then he quit. That's how it always went. After a few choice words from Ricki, he'd calm down. Eventually one of the teachers came by and made him play kickball with a group across the playground.

When the bell rang, Ben and Randall took off to rejoin the boys.

"Schuyler is awful." Vanessa wrinkled her nose.

"He'd shut up if people didn't fall apart," said Ricki. "Kimberly can't help it."

"Sure she can. But maybe she likes being teased."

"That's a dumb thing to say!" Vanessa cried. "She hates it."

"You're calling me dumb? When the rest of you just stand there and shudder when Schuyler acts up? Oh, right! I didn't see *you* stand up for Kimberly. You made *me* do it!"

"He listens to you," said Vanessa.

"I'm sick of defending everybody. *You* do it next time."

Vanessa crossed her arms. "Well, I'm sick of having to cover for you when you forget to do things, or get too busy or lazy."

"Oh. Now I see what you're upset about. The posters."

"Of course I am! I shouldn't have let you have one of mine. You should have made one yourself."

Ricki sighed. "It's not like it's schoolwork. It's just a poster for a Halloween carnival, for dumb Courtney's committee."

"Then why did you promise to do it?" Vanessa demanded. "You hardly ever follow through, except in sports, and that's because if you don't show up for practice they'll kick you off the team."

"And I suppose you're Ms. Perfect," Ricki said acidly.

"I get things done."

"Fine and dandy, but there's more to life. Like, if it weren't for me, you wouldn't have any other friends. You rely on me to make friends for you. Then you expect me to stick up for them all!"

"I would, too, have other friends," said Vanessa.

"Would not."

"Would, too."

Suddenly the girls realized that the boys behind them were listening and laughing at them. They fell quiet. Vanessa blushed in embarrassment. The argument would have to wait.

Somehow, though, they never really finished the argument. Things got too busy.

On the night of the Halloween carnival, Ricki picked up the extension phone in her room and punched in Vanessa's number.

"Are you home . . . alone?" she murmured in a deep voice.

"Oh, yeah, I'm really scared, Ricki." Vanessa gave her best bored sigh.

Ricki chuckled, then whispered, "Are you ready for our parents' Date Number Two?"

"I'm nervous, aren't you? We have to be careful to keep this from being a repeat of the picnic," Vanessa whispered back.

"Right. But don't worry," said Ricki. "It was brilliant of us to invite our parents to the carnival. They'll have so much fun they won't even have a chance to talk, much less argue."

"But people are supposed to talk on dates and get to know each other, aren't they?" Vanessa chewed nervously on her cheek.

"Shoot, Vee. Our parents have known each other for almost three years. Who needs to talk?"

"Keep your fingers crossed," Vanessa said. "I have to go now. Mrs. Quan is helping me finish the hem of my costume."

Vanessa had decided to be Hildegard von Bingen, a composer from the 1100s who was also a painter, a scientist, and a nun.

Personally, Ricki thought that was about the nuttiest costume she'd ever heard of.

"Ricki, what are you going to be? Tell me. You know all about my costume. It isn't fair."

"Life isn't fair, Vee. Good-bye."

Ricki let out a breath. She couldn't tell Vanessa what she was planning to be for Halloween, because she herself didn't know yet. All afternoon she had been scrounging around the condo for odds and ends that might make a costume—maybe a two-headed alien or a squid. Every year Ricki had grand ideas but always waited until the last minute to put her costume together.

Better let Vanessa think it was just a big secret.

Maybe, Ricki thought, Vanessa had a little, tiny point about her habit of, well . . . putting things off. Or maybe Vanessa had a big point.

She sighed and dragged an old black shawl from the back of the hall closet. It would make a good vampire cape. Ricki wrinkled her nose. How boring. People always went as vampires or witches or ghosts when they couldn't think of anything better. If only she had gotten started sooner. . . .

Oh, well. She and her mom had to meet Vanessa and Andy at the carnival in an hour and a half. Vampire, it would have to be.

*   *   *

68

Vanessa watched her father take slow, blissful bites of a hot dog with all the trimmings.

"Yuck," she said, "how can you eat chili on a hot dog? That's got to be the most disgusting food combination ever invented."

They stood near the carnival snack booths on the Kennedy Intermediate playground, where people milled around for the PTA's hot dogs, popcorn, candy apples, and black cat muffins. Others competed in a jack-o'-lantern carving contest.

"It's delicious." Andy held the paper-wrapped hot dog out to Vanessa. "Here, try some."

Vanessa turned her face away. "Ugh! Forget it! Anyway, that chili would drip all over my costume." She smoothed the folds of the long blue robe Mrs. Quan had helped her sew. Suzanne had given her a tasseled gold cord to belt it with and a white scarf to tie around her hair.

"Well," Andy mumbled through a mouthful, "a little dribble of chili and a smudge or two of mustard would add just the right touch."

"I'm sure." Vanessa pursed her lips, scanning the crowd for Ricki and her mother, who were ten minutes late. Fortunately, Andy hadn't seemed to notice yet. He had a thing about punctuality.

At least the weather was perfect for Halloween. A crisp breeze stirred fallen leaves. Wispy clouds veiled a low yellow moon. It could even be called romantic, in a mysterious sort of way.

Just then she spotted Ricki and Anita. "Oh, here they come!"

Andy quickly swallowed the last of his hot dog. Vanessa noticed him carefully wipe his mustache and beard.

69

"Well, hello!" Anita greeted them.

"Hi Anita, Ricki." Andy smiled.

Anita smiled, too, but not at Andy. "Fabulous costume, Vanessa. Oh, I mean, Hildegard! You must have worked very hard."

"Thanks." Vanessa held her arms out and looked down at her robe. "I had a lot of help."

"You're a vampire, Ricki, right?" Andy asked.

"Of course I'm a vampire!" Ricki bared her teeth, showing the gum-machine plastic fangs she had found in her dresser drawer.

"Ee-uu! Yuck!" Vanessa giggled. "You look awful!"

"Thanks!" Ricki wore black pants, a black turtleneck, and the black shawl draped like a cape. Down the sides of her mouth she had painted red lipstick bloodstains. "You two are boring," she told her mom and Andy. "You should've worn costumes."

Andy shrugged. "What's the point? You kids would have us beat hands down."

Vanessa saw Kimberly in a Cinderella costume walk by with her mother. Dani and Louise Ann, dressed as bumblebees, were at the "fishing" booth with their parents trying to win stuffed animals.

Andy and Anita went on talking about all the costumes. It was weird, Vanessa thought, that the two of them weren't talking directly to each other—only to Ricki and her.

Ricki didn't look worried about it. Maybe she was right, and their parents didn't need conversation but just a good time together.

Vanessa looked at her watch. "It's almost time for trick or treating in the classrooms. We'd better go over there."

The breezeways quickly became a madhouse of monsters, goblins, and devils. Kids dashed around to all the

70

different rooms where teachers waited for trick or treaters. Some teachers had set up their rooms to be really spooky, with blinking black lights, cobwebs, and tapes of scary sounds like creaking doors and ghostly laughs.

Andy and Anita waited outside each classroom while Ricki, Vanessa, Kimberly, Louise Ann, and Dani went in as a group. At one point, Ricki noticed Andy had struck up a conversation with Dani's parents. Then Louise Ann's mother came up to talk with Anita. At this rate, Anita and Andy would never have a moment alone. Maybe it was better that way, Ricki decided. No chance for an argument.

When the girls finally walked into their own classroom at the end of the breezeway, they found it pitch dark. Not a sound anywhere. Clinging tightly to each other's hands, they moved slowly into the room.

"Ouch!" Louise Ann cried.

Kimberly shrieked.

"What is it?" Ricki demanded.

"Ran into a desk," said Louise Ann.

"Maybe," Dani whispered, "Mr. Sambucchio forgot the trick or treat."

Vanessa tried to focus. "But how could he? He—"

A bloodcurdling scream tore through the darkness.

All five girls screamed, too, and flew into a giant huddle.

Then the lights came on.

"Happy Halloween, my dears." Mr. Sambucchio sat behind his desk in his yellow bow tie, grinning ear to ear.

"Oh, my gosh!" Kimberly gasped.

"You scared us near to death!" Louise Ann giggled.

Dani smiled delightedly. "Me, too!"

"Well, that was the idea." Mr. Sambucchio smiled back.

"We might just have to get you back someday," Ricki warned.

"If we survive tonight," Vanessa said, clutching at her heart.

Mr. Sambucchio shook his head. "All's fair on Halloween. Your treats are in the basket by the door, girls. Now don't tell the fresh victims, all right?"

They all swore to secrecy and scurried out, giggling.

They didn't get very far, though, because the second they reached the breezeway, another scream ripped at their ears.

Chapter 8

Ricki whirled to find three things: Vanessa turning flame red, Kimberly trying to fish something out of the back of Vanessa's robe, and Schuyler Simmons standing behind them both, snickering.

Ricki rushed forward, not knowing exactly what to yell at Schuyler for but knowing it had to be something.

Before she could say a word, Kimberly pulled a slimy green rubber bait worm from Vanessa's dress, and Vanessa cried out in a high-pitched, quavering voice, "Schuyler Simmons! You—! You'd better never try anything like that again!"

Ricki stared at her friend in shock. Was that really Vanessa Shepherd talking?

Schuyler shrugged. "Hey, you heard what the teacher said. All's fair on Halloween!" He cast a wary glance at Ricki, then down the breezeway at the group of parents, who so far hadn't noticed a thing.

Ricki decided it wasn't the parents he had to watch out for, anyway. She had never seen Vanessa so mad. Her pointy chin thrust forward, and her green eyes blazed. It took a lot to make Vanessa angry, Ricki knew, but once you did, look out!

Schuyler seemed to get the message. His milky blue eyes went wide. He took a couple of slow steps away, then turned around and slunk off like a wet cat.

73

As the girls returned to the bunch of parents, Vanessa started to calm down. She was still angry but felt happy, too. For the first time ever she had stood up for herself, just as Ricki said she should. And Ricki had noticed. She gave Vanessa a big, nonstop grin.

"Hey, you all look like you saw a ghost!" Andy said when they walked up.

"Well, get ready for more," warned Louise Ann's mother, Mrs. Robbins. "Isn't it time for the spook house?"

"Great!" Andy whooped. "Love a good spook house!"

"So do I," Anita agreed, smiling.

Ricki and Vanessa exchanged glances.

They all headed for the auditorium, where a crew of teachers and parents greeted them at a door hung with a sign that read *House of Horrors* in squiggly red letters.

"Now remember," cackled Ms. Abbott, disguised as a witch, "just keep strolling through. Don't rush or try to turn back. Terrible fates await those who disobey!"

The girls all held their parents' hands as they passed under the black drape.

"Oh, my gosh!" Kimberly squealed at the eerie music.

From then on, there was nothing but squealing, giggling, and shrieking. In a mazelike passage, they passed mummies and skeletons and ran into clingy cobwebs. Then, in a room ringed with smoke from dry ice, they had to put their hands into vats of guts and eyeballs.

"It's only spaghetti and grapes, Dani," explained Louise Ann when her friend couldn't stop yelping.

"Having a pleasant evening?" Andy asked Anita. He hunched over and rubbed his hands together like a mad scientist.

"Delightful!" Anita laughed.

Vanessa and Ricki stepped aside together.

"Still have your fingers crossed?" Vanessa whispered.

Ricki nodded. "But maybe we don't need to anymore."

"I know. They're starting to—"

Vanessa was interrupted by a scream.

"Not again." Ricki rolled her eyes.

"Help!" the scream continued. "Help!"

"Where is that coming from?" Dani asked.

Andy grinned. "Frankenstein lurking about."

"No." Mrs. Robbins frowned. "I'm on the PTA committee, and this isn't anything I know about. No part of the spook house plan."

Anita frowned, too. "Then what—"

"Please, help me!" the voice wailed.

Suddenly the spook house music stopped and from outside came shouts and cries of, "What's going on in there?"

"Look!" Andy pointed at a bulge in the black and silver fabric that made up the room's walls—a bulge that was shaking and shivering.

"Someone's stuck!" cried Anita, moving toward the bulge.

Andy followed.

Together they worked to tear the fabric away from its wooden frame, but it wouldn't budge.

"Wait!" Andy used his car keys to punch a small hole in the cloth. Then he and Anita grabbed the fabric and pulled. It made an awful ripping sound.

Ricki, Vanessa, and the others watched aghast as the cloth opened to reveal a large, trembling angel.

"I went the wrong way." The angel's halo quivered.

Anita loosened one of its white feathered "wings" from the wooden frame of the spook house wall.

"Oh, my gosh!" Kimberly gasped. "It's . . . it's Courtney!"

The girls all stared in shock at the angel.

Then Vanessa and Ricki had to work hard not to laugh. It was the first time they had ever felt sorry for Courtney Haines.

"Did you see how well they worked together?" Vanessa whispered into the phone on Saturday morning.

"They ran right to Courtney's rescue!" Ricki whispered on her end of the line. "No arguments about what to do. A real team."

"Oh, Ricki, why can't they see it—how great they'd be together? I mean, will we have to just come right out and tell them?"

Ricki lay on her bed upside down and propped her feet up on the headboard. "The carnival was just last night, Vee. Let's give them time. Maybe they'll figure it out on their own."

Curled up in her rocker, Vanessa sighed. "I suppose you're right. But at this rate—"

"I know. We won't be sisters till we're about forty-two!"

"Not even by Christmas. Oh, that reminds me. I have to get off the phone. My grandparents are going to call."

Not more than a minute after Vanessa hung up, the phone rang.

"Vanessa, dear!" The voice was clear, smooth, and beautiful.

Vanessa got a warm shiver. Her grandmother sounded so much like her mother sometimes. "Hi, Nona. How are you?"

"Oh, darling, we've missed you. Papa and I think of you especially often this month because of Thanksgiving. How we'd love to have you here. Oh, how we'd love to have you here for all holidays, as it was when you were small."

Vanessa imagined her grandmother on the other end of the line: snowy white hair twisted elegantly atop her head, shell pink lipstick and nail gloss perfectly applied, and eyes misting over. Nona could be prim and no-nonsense in person, but on long-distance she got mushy.

"I miss you, too, Nona." Vanessa felt her own eyes misting up. "Is Papa okay?"

"We're both fit as fiddles. And speaking of holidays, Vanessa, do you know if Daddy has made the arrangements for your Christmas visit yet?"

"I don't think so, Nona. He's still calling the airlines."

Nona gave a little snort. "He's being stubborn as usual, you know. If he would just let us take care of the tickets, he wouldn't have to search heaven and earth for a bargain. In any case, we can hardly wait to see you, and neither can Folly. The poor little dog misses you wretchedly, even after all these years."

"Oh, rub her chin for me, Nona." Vanessa adored her grandparents' old Shetland sheepdog, born the same year she was.

At the moment, though, Vanessa was thinking of another subject she wanted to ask Nona about. The words on her mind wouldn't come into her mouth. Sometimes it was a little hard to ask about her mother, where she was and how she was doing.

"I have a new photo of Folly to send you," Nona was saying. "And speaking of photos, I have lovely news. A friend of ours living in Hawaii sent us a marvelous newspaper article from *The Honolulu Star-Bulletin* about your mother, complete with a photograph."

"Really?" Vanessa grew a smile.

"The article is a glowing review of Celeste's singing,"

77

Nona reported. "They call her a 'nightingale.' Isn't that lovely? She's appearing in a hotel doing old 1940s love ballads and such. I've mailed a copy to you."

"Mama wrote me a letter from Hawaii when she first got there in the summer," Vanessa told Nona. "But I haven't heard from her since."

"Did she say if she'd be coming home soon?" Nona asked. Her tone was the prim, no-nonsense one.

"No," replied Vanessa.

"No, she never does, does she," Nona said. "Are you missing her, Vanessa?"

"I—I don't know, Nona. I guess I do, sometimes. But I think I'm used to her being away."

Nona sighed. "Yes, I suppose you are. Well, my darling, here's your grandfather. He's itching to talk with you."

After a chat with Papa, it was time to go. Vanessa blew kisses to him and Nona over the phone, then hung up. And felt miserable. She wished they could have stayed on a little longer. Forever, maybe. Then she would never feel so lonely after hanging up.

Vanessa rocked in her chair. She thought back to how things were before her parents' divorce. The three of them lived in a little apartment in Boston and always visited her grandparents on weekends. Her mother had small, soft hands that smelled of rosewater. Most of the time Celeste was sunny and bright, but other times she wasn't. She cried a lot. She cried even more when she got a chance to sing in nightclubs, and Nona and Papa didn't want her to. Then, worst of all, Celeste and Andy started arguing. Andy believed Celeste shouldn't let her parents rule her life. There were other reasons, too, Vanessa's father explained later, why they eventually had to part.

In her letters Celeste always tried to explain why she

couldn't live close to Vanessa or visit more often. The entertainment business was tough, and she had to stay on the road. And she felt that she still had too much growing up to do herself to be able to raise a child. Vanessa understood, kind of. But she wished she could see her mother more.

She got up from her chair to gaze out the window at a foggy November day. Her father was busy in the living room finishing up the music his band would tape for a movie about mountain lions. And Ricki and her mother were spending the weekend at her Uncle Mario's house, filled with family and Mexican food.

If only . . . Vanessa thought for the millionth time, drifting off into her millionth daydream. If only she and Ricki were sisters, then she could be there, too.

"Now leave Ricki alone, kids," Aunt Ruth told her sons. "Stop fighting over her." She wagged one of her short, plump fingers.

Her husband, tall, plump Uncle Mario, scooped up three-year-old Anthony and grabbed six-year-old Carlos by the hand. "You all come and sit at the table for dinner. Stop pulling Ricki apart."

"I don't mind being fought over," Ricki said. "It makes me feel appreciated, like the last piece of pie." She really did enjoy the attention she got as the oldest cousin. The young ones looked up to her sometimes like a guardian angel and sometimes like a giant toy.

"You'll have plenty of occasions to feel like that after your mother lets you start sitting for us." Aunt Ruth's bright blue eyes and dimples joined in a smile. "If you're still crazy enough."

"I'll turn twelve in June," Ricki said, helping Anthony into his high chair. "Only seven months away."

"On the subject of birthdays and craziness," said her

mother, "Mario, you turned my daughter into a maniac with that camera. Did you show your uncle your latest shots, honey?"

Ricki looked at her mother in surprise. Anita actually sounded enthusiastic about the pictures. Maybe even proud.

"They're in my backpack. I'll get them after dinner."

"Meanwhile," said Aunt Laura, "tell us how your plans for that photography class went." Sitting next to Ricki's mom, Aunt Laura looked almost like her twin— same height, long-lashed dark eyes, and curly black hair.

"Great!" Ricki replied. "The teacher, Mrs. McNee, finally called me back. There aren't any other classes for beginners, but she said that after Christmas she'll spend Saturday mornings at the community center on her own work. I can stop by in January and see if I'd like to help her and learn as we go. Also, she has to see if she likes me, too. I mean, she says she wants to make sure I'm serious."

"Of course she'll like you!" Uncle Mario, Aunt Laura, and Aunt Ruth chimed in at once. Then Uncle Mario started giving her pointers on how to put together a portfolio of her best shots.

After that the conversation jumped around, as usual, to a hundred topics: Thanksgiving, which they would all spend at Ricki's grandparents' farm in Stockton; Aunt Laura's new job teaching marine biology at a university in Santa Cruz; and then they talked about Ricki's other aunt, Aunt Marie, and her new boyfriend.

Ricki kept hoping her aunts and uncles would sooner or later get around to teasing her mother, as they usually did, about her boyfriends and the fact that she never had a serious one. Then maybe Ricki could mention the carnival and how much fun they had with Vanessa and Andy, with the emphasis on Andy.

But while listening to the clamor of voices and laughter, Ricki knew in her heart why it had been easy for her mother to get along without serious boyfriends or a new husband. It was the same reason why Ricki herself had gotten along without her father. Having a big, warm family around, she hardly had time to miss him. Usually, the aunts and uncles and cousins and grandparents kind of filled in the gaps.

She sighed. Maybe her mom had decided never to marry again. That would knock Andy—and the Sisters Scheme—right out of the picture!

No one said a word about Anita's boyfriends or lack of them. Instead, the conversation turned to the boring subject of taxes—Anita's favorite. Her eyes lit up whenever she talked about deductions and incomes and losses. That discouraged Ricki even more. How would she and Vanessa ever be able to convince a person like that to get romantic?

After dinner, though, Ricki felt much better about the whole thing. While she and Uncle Mario sat on the sofa looking at her photographs, Anita and Aunt Laura took the kids to the backyard to play on the swing set. Ricki happened to glance out the window and find the most amazing expression on her mother's face. It was Mom's New Boyfriend Look, Ricki was sure. She had seen it only a few times—when her mom first started dating Milton, a nerdy guy from her office who had a crush on her back when Ricki was in fourth grade, and then stuck-up Eric last year. But there it was. Anita was smiling and laughing with her sister, wearing that look.

Wow! She could hardly wait to tell Vanessa.

*　　*　　*

"Are you sure it was a . . . what did you call it?" Vanessa asked on the phone Sunday.

"Her New Boyfriend Look," Ricki answered. "Positive."

"How can we be sure it's about my father?"

"Who else could it be, Vee? Mom isn't seeing anyone else. I would know. Either she'd tell me she's going out, or she would get phone calls, or—" Ricki was interrupted by a "beep" on the line. "Oh, hold on a minute. Another call is coming in. It's the call-waiting thing. I'll be right back."

Ricki switched over to the incoming line. "Hello?"

"Ah. Hello, there. Ah, may I speak with . . . Anita Romero, please?" It was a man's voice. Very deep. Kind of nasal. He sounded fat. And vaguely familiar.

"Sorry, she can't come to the phone now," Ricki said. Actually, Anita had gone down for the newspaper, but Ricki wasn't supposed to say that. "May I take a message?"

"Ah, well, yes. All right. This is Sidney Banks."

Ricki frowned. Sidney Banks? The name sounded familiar, too. Then she remembered. This guy had called once before, last week. Ricki had thought he was one of her mom's clients. Anita got lots of calls from clients during the week. But not on weekends.

"And your phone number?" Ricki asked.

"She has it."

His tone of voice made Ricki's heart sink. "She does?"

"Oh, yes. Ask her to call me, please."

"Oh, um, sure," Ricki said.

Sidney Banks hung up.

"Vee?" Ricki cried after she switched the line back.

"What? What happened?"

"Oh, Vee. It was Sidney!"

Chapter 9

Ricki huddled in her jacket. She watched Vanessa throw off her sweater and dash around with Aunt Laura's dogs as if it were summer.

Aunt Laura had taken them hiking in Mount Tamalpais State Park, where an icy December wind cut across the golden hills and flattened the meadow grasses.

"When are you going to visit your grandparents, Vanessa?" Aunt Laura asked, climbing up onto Ricki's boulder to sit next to her.

"Next week." Vanessa tossed the ball across the meadow for Boss, a big black retriever.

"They have a dog, right?" Aunt Laura asked, reaching down to pet her German shepherd mix, Maggie. "You'll have fun."

"Oh, I know. I love spending Christmas with my grandparents. But sometimes, well . . . it's confusing. I mean, sometimes I'd like to stay home for the holidays. And I always miss Ricki."

Ricki grinned down from her perch. "Me, too. Wouldn't it be fun to have Christmas together?"

"A blast! We could open presents together!"

"That would be great for you, wouldn't it?" Aunt Laura took off her knit cap and fluffed her hair. "Well, maybe someday."

Vanessa looked up from rubbing Maggie's ears. Aunt Laura's voice had sounded funny. And her smile looked funny, too. Vanessa glanced at Ricki, but she was busy wiping dog slobber off her hands. Boss had jumped on her boulder, and the fastest way to get rid of him had been to throw the ball.

Vanessa shrugged. She must have been imagining things.

But later, on the ride home, Aunt Laura asked, "Well, did you guys like the park?"

"Oh, yes," Vanessa said. "It was beautiful."

"Freezing," said Ricki from the backseat, "but beautiful."

"A lot better than our last trip to a park," Vanessa added.

Ricki sighed. "Our picnic with Mom and Andy."

"Oh. Right." Aunt Laura grinned. "I heard about that."

"You did?" Ricki knew her mom must have told her sister all about it, but there was something else in Aunt Laura's voice. . . .

"We were trying to have a family outing," Vanessa said. "You know, do something fun all together."

Aunt Laura nodded. "Nice idea."

"But it didn't work out too well," said Ricki.

"It's hard to get our parents . . . um, together, sometimes," Vanessa continued. "They're so busy and everything."

"Maybe," said Aunt Laura, "you should tell them how you feel." She pulled into a service station for gas.

The minute she got out of the car, Ricki whispered, "Did you hear that? Mom told her about the picnic and probably the carnival, too. And Aunt Laura wouldn't say

84

we should try to get our parents together more often if Mom had said she hated Andy, would she?''

Vanessa answered, ''There's a big difference between not hating someone and marrying them. And what about Sidney?''

''Oh. I almost forgot. Sidney.''

''Did you ever ask your mom about him?''

''Yeah.'' Ricki sighed. ''I asked her how come a client was calling on Sunday, and she just said they had something to talk about. She looked really cagey.''

For a moment, the girls fell into a glum silence.

Then Vanessa said, ''Look, Ricki. Who cares about Sidney? I mean, whoever he is, my father is ten times better, right?''

''Hey, right!'' Ricki agreed. ''I hadn't thought of that. Your dad has got to be a *hundred* times better. Plus, he's not fat. I think Sidney's fat. Mom goes for the more athletic types. Like my father. He was a minor league baseball player before they got married.''

''Really?''

''Yeah. And then he bought a ranch, so he had to be even more athletic then. Mom, too. Hard work, she says. I don't remember, because I was just a baby when we lived there, but . . .''

''Ricki, my father is not athletic.''

Ricki frowned. ''Well, he could be. I mean, if he wanted to.''

''He doesn't have big muscles or anything.''

''True, but looks aren't everything, Vee. Anyway, he's not bad looking. He's kind of cute.''

''What we need to do is point that out to your mother,'' Vanessa said. ''And point out to Dad how great *she* is. We can't let this Sidney thing stop us, right?''

Aunt Laura came back to the car and got in. "We're tanked and ready to roll, folks."

Grinning at Vanessa, Ricki made a thumbs-up sign. "Right!"

Vanessa climbed into the string hammock on the back deck of the new house. She and her father, along with Gordon and Suzanne, had just rigged the hammock up.

"My, you look comfortable," Suzanne said, smiling. A paint-smudged headband held back her black hair.

"Well, don't get too comfortable. Let us try it." Gordon helped Vanessa out of the hammock, then he and Suzanne barreled in, laughing when it swung wildly back and forth.

"Ah, the fruits of labor." Andy smiled down at them. "My turn." He pulled Gordon and Suzanne out and settled into the hammock regally, as if it were his throne. "Now, this is living."

Vanessa had to agree that the hammock, an early house-warming present that Suzanne had gotten in Mexico, was a great idea. She could imagine lazy summer afternoons of books and lemonade. But today, barely the beginning of February, was far from summer. And even though Andy had made progress on the house, it was nowhere near ready to be lived in. Just that week he had hired a man to blow in insulation because the place was so cold and damp. The downstairs rooms were all fixed up, and the kitchen and bathrooms actually worked, but the upstairs bedrooms were still disasters.

"All right, King Andrew," said Gordon. "Suze and I gotta go."

"Should we report back for more home improvement duty tonight?" Suzanne asked.

Andy got up. "Nah. You're off the hook. No work

tonight. But thanks for all your help today. And for the hammock, Suzanne.''

"What?" Vanessa raised her eyebrows. "No work tonight? Are you serious, Dad? You're actually giving up a fun Saturday night here?"

He smiled. "Yes, I am. I'm, uh, I'm going out tonight, Vee."

"Oh," she said. "Where?"

"A play. Would you mind staying with Mrs. Quan?"

Vanessa shook her head. "No." Her dad usually took her with him to plays and concerts. She only had to stay with Mrs. Quan if he was playing a gig somewhere, or if . . . Vanessa chewed anxiously on the inside of her cheek. Or if he had a date!

"You're welcome to spend the evening with us, Vanessa," Suzanne offered. "We're going to rent *Amadeus*."

"Well?" Andy asked. "Would you like to do that?"

Vanessa nodded, still worried. "But, I haven't practiced today, and my recital is in three weeks. . . ."

Gordon chuckled. "Bring the cello. At my apartment, heaven knows the neighbors are fully accustomed to the sound of music."

At home that afternoon, Vanessa hurried to her room and dialed Ricki's number. "Please be home, please be home," she whispered.

"Hello?" Anita answered.

"Hi, Anita. Is Ricki there?"

"Good timing, hon. She just got back from the community center."

Ricki finally picked up the phone in her room. "Hi."

"Oh, Ricki, I—"

"Hold on, Vee. Let me change my shirt."

"But Ricki—"

The phone clunked to the floor.

"Okay. I'm back."

"Ricki, listen. I've got news."

"Really? Well, so do I. My session with Mrs. McNee was great today. She showed me how to print pictures from negatives."

"Good, but—" Vanessa began.

"Oh, wait. Sorry," Ricki said. "Let me take off my sock. It's got a hole in the toe that's driving me nuts."

Vanessa sighed.

"Okay, I'm back again. Now, what was it you wanted to say?"

Vanessa let out a groan. "I'm exhausted with the effort, Ricki! Are you going to listen now?"

"Sure."

"I think my father is going on a date."

Ricki let out a little shriek. "A *what*? Why didn't you say so?"

"You wouldn't let me! Oh, Ricki, what are we going to do?"

"We have to stay calm. You say you *think* he's got a date?"

"Yes," Vanessa whispered. "He told me I had to stay with Mrs. Quan tonight because he's going to a play."

"A play? Wow. That must be the 'in' thing this week. Mom's going to one, too."

"Oh." Vanessa sighed again. "Well, Dad goes to lots of plays and small music concerts and things, and most of the time I go with him. Even when I was little, I'd go, although then I'd usually fall asleep. But now I don't, and it's just strange that—"

"He didn't invite you," Ricki said.

"Exactly. And he acted kind of embarrassed about it, too."

"You didn't ask him why?" Ricki questioned.

"No. I should have, shouldn't I? But I'm really sure about this. I could tell by the way he acted."

"That it's really a date?"

"It's really a date," Vanessa answered grimly.

"Bad news," said Ricki.

"Yes. First your mother and Sidney," Vanessa said.

"Now your dad and whoever. Vee, we need action."

"We can't just twiddle our thumbs on this," Vanessa agreed.

"Tell your dad my mom loves to, um, paint or something."

"Varnish wood floors. That's what he's doing now. Upstairs."

"Yeah," Ricki said. "It's true, sort of. I mean, once when I got home from helping you guys at the house, Mom talked about how exciting it must be to renew an old, decrepit home."

"Really? Well, you tell your mother that Dad could use more help. That's absolutely true, too. Almost everyone he knows has been out there. He expects us to move in by April, and I just don't see how, even if the entire city of Berkeley worked on it."

"It won't be very romantic. Getting them together to varnish."

"I know. But we're desperate," Vanessa said. "And anyway, while they're hard at work on the floors, you and I can work on *them*."

Ricki giggled. "Right. Like Aunt Laura said, we'll let them know how we feel."

Ricki's mother settled into one of the cane-back chairs in the Shepherd's new kitchen and stretched her arms up over her head.

"Oh, this is heaven," she said.

"Listen to that, girls." Andy shook his head. "She's been on her hands and knees most of the afternoon, has varnish on her nose, and she calls it heaven."

Anita laughed. "What I meant was this kitchen. I love it. All this sunlight. You did a marvelous job."

Ricki's ears pricked up. Her mother, admiring this kind of kitchen, which was about 180 degrees different from their own black and white, super-modern condo? Andy had put in oak cabinets, a clay tile floor, and a skylight, making it as cozy and warm as a mountain cabin, not at all like the bridge of a starship.

"Well, thank you." Andy set a pitcher of iced mint tea and glasses on the table.

Vanessa brought a bowl of strawberries from the fridge. "This is a reward for the hard work. Dad likes to bribe people with food."

"Homemade nut cake," he said. "And oranges from the garden."

"See what I mean?" Vanessa asked.

"Fine with me." Ricki helped herself to a slice of cake.

The day was going great, she decided. Anita had volunteered her help the minute she heard Andy needed it. No fuss at all about getting together this time. And so far, no arguments, either. The two of them worked on the floors together as well as they had on freeing Courtney from the spook house. To top it off, Anita looked more relaxed and happy than she had since last summer's vacation in San Diego.

Meanwhile, Vanessa felt ecstatic. The four of them sat at the kitchen table like a family. It just had to happen. She could feel it in her bones. She and Ricki had to make it happen.

"Well," she said, picking a strawberry from the bowl.

90

Everyone kept munching.

Vanessa went on. "Anita, Ricki tells me you, um, you like plays."

Ricki aimed a look at her. Hey, Vee, way to be subtle.

"Well, so does Dad," Vanessa said. "Isn't that interesting?"

Ricki's eyes shot to her mom.

Anita smiled and tucked a curl back under her red bandana. "Oh. Yes, in fact. I do."

"More tea, anyone?" Andy asked.

Odd, Vanessa thought. Her father had just poured tea ten seconds ago.

Silence fell over the table. Someone had to keep a conversation going, so Ricki got on Vanessa's track. "You like plays, too, Andy?"

Andy chewed nut cake. "Mmm-hmm."

"Dad just saw one last Saturday," Vanessa commented. "What was it called, Dad?"

Andy took a big gulp of tea, then mumbled, "*The Torch-Bearers*, by George Kelly."

"You saw one Saturday, too, Mom, didn't you?" Ricki smiled in satisfaction. She and Vee were making an excellent point. Their parents both liked going to plays. Even on the same night.

Vanessa stayed with it. "Which play did you see, Anita?"

Ricki's mother looked up. She was still smiling, Ricki noticed, but now it was in a sort of nervous way. She focused on Andy. "I saw *The Torch-Bearers*."

Vanessa clapped her hands. "Wow! Isn't that something?"

"Yeah!" Ricki joined in. "What a coincidence."

"Definitely. That you should both—" Vanessa stopped

midsentence, because she noticed that her father and Anita were looking at each other. Staring, in fact.

But Ricki kept talking. "That you should both see the same play on the same—" Then she stopped, too. "Night," she finished, her voice trailing off.

"It was a good play," Anita said, "and we—"

"We had a great time," said Andy.

"Yes," agreed Anita. "We did."

"We—" Andy began.

He was interrupted.

"We?" cried Vanessa and Ricki.

Their parents wore big, sheepish grins.

Chapter 10

"We didn't want to tell you quite yet," Anita said.

"We thought you might be . . . uncomfortable." Andy ran a hand through his tousled hair. "About our seeing each other."

"We thought you might feel strange about it," continued Anita. "Or awkward, because of your friendship."

"And we wanted to take it one step at a time," Andy added.

After several minutes, Ricki and Vanessa still sat speechless. Vanessa could hear what their parents were saying, but somehow she couldn't take it in. And Ricki just kept thinking, It's happening!

Finally, the girls' eyes met. Each saw astonishment on the other's face. They couldn't help it—first they broke into huge grins, then quiet giggles.

It was their parents' turn to look surprised.

"Hmm," Andy said to Anita. "Do *you* get the joke?"

Anita shook her head. "No. Do you?"

"I'm stumped. Unless it's the giggle disease again."

"I thought they recovered from that in fifth grade," Anita said.

"Maybe not." Andy gazed from one girl to the other, then asked, "Care to let us in on what's so funny?"

Vanessa tried to stop laughing, but it was hard.

The joke, Ricki realized, had been on her and Vee!

"How long have they been seeing each other?" Louise Ann asked at lunch Monday.

"Since early October." Vanessa smiled blissfully. "We're pretty sure it was the picnic that did it."

Kimberly looked puzzled. "But you just told us they had a big fight at the picnic."

"Well, they did," Ricki answered, "but afterward Andy called Mom to apologize, then Mom asked him to lunch." She threw her shoulders back proudly. "Things took off from there. They explained it all to us Saturday."

Vanessa and Ricki brimmed with happiness. They just had to tell their friends all about the Sisters Scheme—and its recent success.

"How wonderful." Dani sighed. "Last week was Valentine's Day!"

"Well-timed, huh?" Ricki said. "But listen, folks, you've got to promise not to tell anyone about this. We can't afford to have our parents find out what we've been up to."

"Right," agreed Vanessa. "We've still got work to do."

"You mean until they get married?" Kimberly asked.

Vanessa nodded. "Until they're even engaged!"

"Cross our hearts." Louise Ann made the sign over her chest.

Dani and Kimberly followed.

"This is so romantic!" Dani's huge dark eyes blinked dreamily.

"But how about that man?" Kimberly asked. "The one you said your mother was dating, Ricki?"

"Sidney," said Vanessa. "Hmm."

"Good old Sidney," Ricki added, then shrugged.

"Actually, that's a good question," Louise Ann pointed out. "What about Sidney? What if your mother is dating him, too, Ricki?"

Vanessa frowned. "Oh, my."

"She wouldn't do that," promised Ricki, reaching for one of Kimberly's potato chips. "Anyway, Sidney's a nerd."

"How do you know?" asked Kimberly.

"I just do." Ricki crunched hard on the chip.

Vanessa knew what that tone of voice meant. It was Ricki's worried-but-trying-not-to-show-it voice.

Neither of them worried much, though, about the mysterious Sidney, because the next couple of weeks went so well.

Andy, Anita, and Ricki attended Vanessa's cello recital together Friday night. Ricki got the strong feeling that the four of them were already a family, all tuned in and mentally crossing their fingers for Vanessa's performance. Vee looked like a real pro on the stage in her lacy white blouse, long black skirt, and blond hair pulled neatly back with a black satin ribbon. Her face stayed calm and pretty as always—even a little dreamy, Ricki decided.

Vanessa, though, felt anything but calm or dreamy. Mostly, she wondered what on earth she was doing on that stage. Her stomach tied itself in knots, and her fingers froze while she waited for her part of the program. But that's how she always felt at recitals, even though she had given one twice a year since she was six.

As usual, when her name and first piece were announced, she drew a good, solid breath and let it out. Then she sat in the solo chair and positioned her old, familiar cello between her knees. Her stomach knots slowly loosened, and her fingers thawed. The bow became a friend and partner in her hand.

For just a second, she glanced out at the audience and caught sight of Suzanne, Gordon, and Mrs. Quan in the front row. Her father, Ricki, and Anita sat behind them. Vanessa smiled. And in the split second before she nodded at her teacher, Mr. Matsuro, to accompany her on the piano, she noticed something.

Her father and Anita were holding hands!

That fact gave her first piece, a fast Spanish folk song, quite a bit of extra zip.

"What should I do with these reject prints, Mrs. McNee?"

Ricki held a stack of a dozen photographs over the darkroom trash bin Saturday morning. She had just spent an hour working on one single negative square, placing it on the enlarger over and over, trying to get the shading just right. Mrs. McNee had explained earlier that the enlarger shone light through the transparent negative film to mark the photograhic print paper underneath with an image.

At the moment, it all sounded like mumbo jumbo to Ricki. She was sick of making prints.

"You don't want to throw those away, dear," said Mrs. McNee in her brisk Scottish accent. She batted a string of peppery gray hair off her cheek, then turned back to her own prints at the enlarger station next to Ricki's.

"Why not?" Ricki asked. "They're crummy."

Mrs. McNee frowned at Ricki over the rims of her thick glasses. "Why are they crummy, Ricki?"

"That contrast thing you talked about. These prints came out in shades of gray. They're not strong-looking, like you said."

"I agree. The contrast could be richer. But this is a very nice shot to begin with." Mrs. McNee peered at the negative through her glasses. "Who is it, dear, your sister?"

Ricki grinned. "Not exactly. My best friend. Here she's playing the cello at her recital. I want this as a present for her."

"I see. Well, let me show you a trick or two." Mrs. McNee huffed a little as she heaved off her wooden stool.

Ricki tried to pay attention as Mrs. McNee adjusted the enlarger, but her brain kept tuning out. She thought about softball starting next month, and the little brown age spots on the back of Mrs. McNee's hand, and the Chinese take-out her mom was bringing home for dinner.

Underneath it all, she felt bored with photography. She'd been coming to the community center every Saturday morning since the end of Christmas vacation—nearly two months. It was hard work. First she had to help Mrs. McNee process her film, then work on her own photographs. She really liked Mrs. McNee, and Mrs. McNee was super-nice about explaining things to her. But . . . it was getting to be a real drag spending every Saturday morning cooped up in the photo lab doing the same old things. Maybe she should quit.

Vanessa, she knew, would accuse her of goofing off. Ricki could almost hear her saying, "You never follow through!"

But this photography stuff wasn't anything like what Ricki had imagined—the glamorous lives of photographers on TV, snapping shots of the White House or of volcanoes or movie stars.

"Now," Mrs. McNee was saying, "you see how the contrast improves?"

"Oh, uh, yeah." Ricki focused on the new print.

It showed a girl on a stage, bow poised on the strings of her cello, frowning in concentration, but sort of glowing, too.

It was Vanessa, perfectly Vanessa, exactly how she had looked on the night of the recital. "That's it!" Ricki cried.

"Yes. Very nice, isn't it? It captures a mood."

Ricki held the print up to the light. She found all kinds of feelings in the picture—Vanessa's excitement, her deep concentration, even the years of cello practice that went into her performance.

Ricki grinned at Mrs. McNee. Maybe that was what this photography stuff was all about.

Three dozen tropical fish drifted about under Vanessa's nose. She and Ricki peered down into the aquarium at The Happy Carrot Health Café while their parents ordered.

"I'd love to have a big aquarium like this," Vanessa said. "It's beautiful. About four feet long, don't you think?"

Ricki squatted to look at a blue fish at eye level. "Yeah. What kind is this one?"

"Oh, that's a tang," said Vanessa. "Isn't it beautiful?"

"You can have a big tank at the new house, can't you?"

Vanessa nodded. "I have a spot picked out. You know that wall between the bookcases in the den? It's protected from drafts, and there's just enough light. I can sit in the den and read, with my dog at my feet, and look up now and then at my fish. . . ."

"You mean, you finally have something good to say about living in that house?" Ricki pretended to fall over backward. "I'm shocked."

Vanessa kept her eyes on a damselfish. "It does mean

I'll get to have a dog, and an aquarium, maybe a cat or two, and—"

"Wait. You're actually beginning to sound excited, Vee."

Vanessa pursed her lips. "I'll admit. I am a teeny, tiny bit excited. Sort of. In a way."

"Oh, okay. Just a teeny, tiny bit. Sort of. In a way. I wouldn't want you to get over-enthusiastic."

Vanessa gave Ricki a playful shove. "Oh, go away."

Ricki glanced around the café. "You know, there are about as many different kinds of people in here as there are fish in the tank."

Vanessa watched a woman in a blue silk Indian sari dress float by. The cashier, sitting under a huge wall mural of the constellations, had purple hair. A teenage guy in line wore tie-dyed overalls and a silver ring through one nostril. And at a table by the window sat a man in a hunter's camouflage outfit.

"I think," Ricki whispered, "that you, me, Mom, and your dad are the only normal folks in here."

"Then that makes us abnormal, doesn't it?" Vanessa pointed out.

Ricki shrugged. "Guess so. Never thought of it that way."

Ricki liked The Happy Carrot. Andy often brought her and Vanessa there for frozen yogurt. They always ran into his artist friends, who sat around for hours arguing about somebody's sculpture or looking moody while drinking herbal tea. But Ricki wondered if she'd ever get used to being around odd-looking people, like Vanessa was. And how about her mother, who never left the house wearing anything more unusual than neatly pressed blue jeans? What did she think about The Happy Carrot—and Andy's friends?

Ricki's eyes glued onto a tall man wearing a white turban.

She felt a poke in the ribs. Vanessa whispered, "Look at them. Aren't they just, well . . . beautiful?"

Ricki sighed. "Yes, Vee. The fish are beautiful. You've already said that a million—"

"No! Not the fish. Look at our *parents*."

Ricki looked. Andy, wearing one of his cute little-boy grins, held his arm tenderly around her mother's shoulders. Anita snuggled in close.

"I can't believe this," Ricki whispered.

Vanessa shook her head. "Neither can I."

"Before they told us their secret, I had begun to give up."

"Me, too," Vanessa confessed. "Nothing we tried seemed to work."

"But it did work."

Vanessa nodded. "Except—"

"We're still not sisters," Ricki finished.

"Even though things have been going so well," Vanessa went on. "Today, for instance, your mother came to pick you up, and instead of us begging for more time together, she and Dad were the ones who couldn't seem to part!"

"So we ended up having dinner together. It's happened three times this month. Wouldn't it be a lot easier if they just—"

"Went ahead and got married!" Vanessa exclaimed. "It's obvious that they're in love. Desperately in love."

"A tempestuous romance!" Ricki clutched her hands over her heart dramatically. "Just like the book said, right?"

Vanessa giggled. "We should have read the rest of it.

100

Maybe there's a chapter called 'Convincing People to Get Married.' ''

''Vee, why don't we just ask them?''

''Ask them to get married? That would be like us proposing to them. They're supposed to propose to each other.''

Ricki shrugged. ''Yeah, but remember what Aunt Laura said? About letting them know how we feel?''

Vanessa raised an eyebrow. ''They did seem really worried that day when they confessed about dating. I mean, that we'd be upset or something. Maybe we should ease their minds.''

Ricki nodded. ''Yeah! That is, in a subtle way.''

''Right.'' Vanessa grinned. ''We're good at that, aren't we?''

The girls looked at each other and cracked up laughing.

''Well, you do it this time, Ricki. I was the one who did all the work at the new house that day.''

''Me? What should I say?''

''Oh, um, how about—'' Vanessa frowned. ''Oh, no, wait! I just thought of something. What if . . . well, what about Sidney?''

''What about Sidney?''

''What if your mother really is dating him, too, like Louise Ann said?'' Vanessa asked. ''Maybe that's why she won't marry my father. I mean, maybe Dad has already proposed to her and everything, but she's too busy dating someone else, and—''

''What? That's the dumbest thing I've ever heard. What if your dad is too busy dating one of those artist women— that Zinka or something. I bet Mom has already proposed to him, but—''

''Her name is Zinna,'' Vanessa corrected, hand on hip,

"and my father does not date her. That is dumb. And how do you know if—"

Andy interrupted her. "Girls! The salads are here," he called from the table.

Ricki crossed her arms. "You get some pretty dumb ideas, Vee."

"Well, so do you," replied Vanessa. "Anyway, it's your turn to do something."

Ricki snorted. "Great. Just great."

At the table, Ricki sat down feeling nervous. The fate of the whole family seemed to rest on her shoulders. What could she possibly say to make wedding bells chime?

Looking at her salad made her feel even more nervous. There was a mountain of alfalfa sprouts with about seventeen mushroom slices teetering on the summit. She hated mushrooms.

Vanessa helpfully forked off the top half of the mountain to her own bowl. Ricki smiled a thank-you. Vanessa smiled back. Making up with Vee after arguments was always easy.

"Ricki," Andy said between swallows of his carrot juice. "When's your first softball game with the parks league this season?"

"Next week. Do you think you might come?"

"Hey, you can bet on it! I really enjoyed it last year."

Anita and Andy started talking about baseball and the World Series of 1989 across the bay in San Francisco, which was interrupted by a big earthquake.

Vanessa thought back to another earthquake, the day when her father and Anita helped drive her and Ricki's class to The Exploratorium museum. Never in her life had she felt more frightened than when the whole building shook and trembled around them. Andy and Anita stayed perfectly calm, though, rounding up all the kids and carefully counting heads.

Hah! thought Vanessa. There was something else her dad and Anita had in common. Not only did they both love baseball, but they both stayed calm during emergencies. Quaky museum visits, fake angels stuck in spook houses . . . Vanessa realized this would be a perfect point in the conversation to work on the Sisters Scheme.

She kicked Ricki under the table. "Ow!" Ricki yelped.

Anita frowned at her. "What is it, honey?"

"Oh. Uh," Ricki mumbled. "Nothing. I, uh, bit down too hard on a sunflower seed."

Anita patted Ricki's shoulder. "Well, be careful. Last year I broke a filling eating Cornnuts. Can you imagine? It was painful. Oh, and the dentist's bill was enormous."

Andy nodded. "Yup, I can imagine. And on Cornnuts. Ugh. You eat those? What a way to go."

He and Anita launched into a discussion of nutrition and started comparing dentists, while Vanessa and Ricki exchanged looks.

Ricki had an idea but didn't know what to do with it. If only she had more time to think. Now or never, she finally decided.

"Mom?" she said during a lull in the conversation.

"Mmm?" Anita shook salt on her spinach omelet.

"I was wondering. . . . Aren't family dental plans cheaper?"

"Cheaper than what, hon?"

"Well," Ricki said, "cheaper than if you have two separate plans. I mean, for four people who could be on one plan."

Anita frowned in bewilderment.

"You mean," Andy jumped in, "if four people go in

on one dental insurance plan together, instead of being on separate ones.'' He grinned a little.

"Yeah. Right.'' Ricki tried to signal an SOS to Vanessa with her eyes. Just to be sure, she gave Vanessa a kick under the table.

"Ouch! Um, yes,'' Vanessa piped up. "Lots of things could be cheaper, couldn't they? Um, insurance, rent, phone bills . . .''

"And don't forget gasoline and groceries,'' Ricki added.

Anita set her fork down. "Girls, are you trying to say something?''

Ricki and Vanessa looked at each other. "Who, us?''

"Yes,'' Andy answered, "you.''

Ricki shrugged. "We just . . .''

"We were just wondering. . . .'' Vanessa began, but chickenend out.

Finally, Ricki couldn't stand the suspense. "When are you getting married?''

Chapter 11

"Ricki!" Vanessa cried in horror, then kicked her. "Ow!"

Andy frowned. "Are you girls kicking each other?" Ricki rubbed her shin.

Vanessa said, "What Ricki meant to say was—"

"We need to tell you something, girls," Anita interrupted.

Andy nodded. "Anita's right."

"We've been seeing a couples counselor," said Anita.

Andy said, "We really want to get started on the right foot."

"Get what started on the right foot?" Vanessa asked.

"Well," began Anita, "every relationship has a few rocky spots in the beginning, and Dr. Banks says that—"

"Wait," Ricki said. She cocked an ear at her mother. "Dr. who?"

Andy smiled. "Dr. Banks. I call him Sid, but your mom is more respectful."

"Sid?" Vanessa asked. "Sidney?"

"Hey! Sidney Banks!" Ricki stuck her tongue out at Vanessa. "See!"

"See what?" Anita wanted to know.

Andy tapped his knife lightly on a glass to get their attention. "Listen, my dears. The important thing is that Anita and I . . . we have grown very close. . . . And . . . we're very happy."

"But your happiness is important to us, too," Anita said. "We don't want you to feel left out of our decisions. We're thinking about—"

"Getting married!" the girls sang together.

It was true. No daydream or fantasy. Vanessa's father and Ricki's mother really were on their way to the altar. Or, at least, Vanessa reminded herself Thursday night, they were thinking about it, which was definitely a step in the right direction.

She planted her marker between pages of a book on sea otters that Ricki's Aunt Laura had given her along with a promise to take her and Ricki snorkeling in Monterey Bay.

Someday, Ricki's Aunt Laura might be her aunt, too, Vanessa realized, nestling into the living room sofa. She would be able to share Ricki's whole family—all the aunts, uncles, cousins, and grandparents.

That was something to look forward to. Vanessa didn't have many relatives herself. Andy's parents died before she was born and had no children except him. On his side, there was just Great Aunt Allegra in North Carolina. And her mama's parents lived far away in Boston.

If Andy and Anita were to marry, Vanessa would gain a whole new family overnight. And Ricki as a sister, finally! Plus, something she hadn't really thought about before—Anita as a stepmother.

Vanessa didn't feel she needed a mother, even though she did miss hers sometimes. Andy made a pretty good parent alone. Still, it might be nice to have a stepmother.

Wouldn't it?

Things were turning out just as she and Ricki had planned. All that they had worked for was coming true. Then why, Vanessa wondered, did she have such a nervous, worried feeling?

"Okay, Romero," Coach Jenkins said to Ricki, scratching his big belly. "Looks like there's a hole in left field."

"Right, Coach." Ricki got up from the dugout bench and grabbed a bat from the rack. It was the Berkeley Bobcats' first game and her first time at bat that season. Her heartbeat sped up a little.

Coach gave her a jowly grin and a clap on the back. "Get a hit!"

Her teammates Marc Ortega and Julie Steinberg clapped her on the back, too, as Ricki trotted out to the batter's box. Crouching in position, she cocked the bat over her shoulder. In a quick glance at the bleachers she spotted her mom, Vanessa, and Andy.

"Go get 'em, slugger!" Andy called, waving his orange and black San Francisco Giants cap in the air like a flag for her.

"That your fan club, Pigtails?" yelled a boy from the other team.

Ricki fought a blush and kept her eyes on the pitcher.

The ball came at her low and hard. She swung and heard a solid crack.

"All right!" Coach Jenkins hollered. "Go for two!"

Ricki dashed toward first base and saw her ball roll out of the outfielder's reach. She rounded first and sprinted for second base. In a cloud of dust, she slid in.

Ricki panted happily. She got up and dusted herself off.

Not bad for a first swing. She kept her eyes off the bleachers, though, worried that Andy might start cheering again.

Funny, she thought, that there she was on second base, and you could say that was where the Sisters Scheme was, too. Anita and Andy's dating had been first base. Thinking about marriage was second. They'd make it to third when they got engaged, then slide into home at the wedding.

The four of them would move in together at the new house, where there would be no more frozen dinners. Andy and Vanessa never had frozen anything. They didn't even own a microwave. Ricki sighed. She and her mom would definitely have to bring their own.

Looking on the bright side, Andy would probably come to all her home games with Anita. At least, that was mostly on the bright side. The cap waving, Ricki could do without. It was embarrassing. But it would be great to have a father-type person around.

Wouldn't it?

Waiting for the next batter, Ricki got a sudden flash to some of the fathers on old TV show reruns: Mr. Cleaver on "Leave it to Beaver," Mr. Brady on "The Brady Bunch." They were the take-control, "I'm the boss" kind of dads.

Andy wouldn't be that way, would he? Nah, Ricki decided. Andy was a great guy. He'd be a great stepdad.

Wouldn't he?

"We're here!" Anita called as she and Ricki rushed up the stairs of the Shepherd's new house Saturday afternoon. "I'm really sorry we're late, folks."

Andy set his paintbrush on the rim of a bucket and gave Anita a hello peck when she entered the master bedroom.

Ricki decided he looked terrible. Gray bags hung under his eyes.

She said hi to Vanessa, then inspected the bedroom's new windows.

"Looks great," she told Vanessa. "But what's wrong with your dad? He looks like a zombie."

"Last night he had a gig that lasted till 3:00 A.M., and we've been working here since ten this morning."

"That'll do it." Ricki nodded.

Anita was still apologizing. "I had to go into the office and catch up on paperwork, which I thought I'd have done by two." She glanced at her watch. "Oh, my goodness. It's nearly four. I truly am sorry, Andy. Well, doesn't this look lovely? I'm glad you decided on the wood frame windows. They're just right. Oh, and the apricot color on the walls is glorious. I really do like it."

"Your mother is even more talkative than usual today," Vanessa whispered to Ricki. "What's wrong with her?"

"Oh, same as your dad. She's tired. She gets chatty when she's worn out. All hyped-up."

Anita dropped her purse to the floor and collapsed in a chair. "I dashed to pick up Ricki at the photo lab, then dashed home to change, and oh! Just let me catch my breath. Then hand me a brush."

Andy never looked up from his painting.

"Just relax, Anita," he finally said in a dry, flat voice.

The girls looked at him.

"What do you mean, 'relax'?" Anita asked. "If we're going to get this room finished . . ."

"Don't worry about it." Now Andy's voice had an edge to it.

"Andy, hon," Anita said, "I rushed over here to help you. In fact, I cut my day short at the office."

Andy just nodded.

Eyes wide, Vanessa watched him and Anita. Ricki held her breath.

"If you're upset because I was late . . ." Anita began.

"Yes," Andy replied. "I am."

"I told you, I'm terribly sorry."

"You're always terribly sorry, Anita. And you're always late."

"Well, pardon me." Anita stood up. "I know that in your mind tardiness is a wicked sin."

"You don't have to get sarcastic." Andy stopped painting.

"Why not? I've already tried apologizing."

Ricki saw that her mother's eyes had narrowed to midnight black slits. There were two bright spots of color on her high cheekbones. She held her shoulders perfectly straight.

Vanessa stared at her father—at the stubborn set of his jaw, the "who cares?" look in his brown eyes, and the way he kept smoothing his mustache with a thumb.

There had to be a way to stop this!

Before either girl had a chance to think, they heard Andy say, "You're tired and on edge, Anita. Maybe you should go home."

Anita yanked the red bandana off her hair. "Well, I think *you're* tired and on edge, Andy. That's why you're being ugly to me."

"I'm not being ugly."

"Yes, you are."

Andy started painting again. Vanessa thought that at any minute she'd see smoke rise from his ears.

"I think I will go now," Anita announced.

"Fine," Andy answered.

"Fine." Anita grabbed her purse from the floor and slung the strap over her shoulder. Then she stomped out of the room.

110

She was halfway down the stairs before she called, "Ricki!"

For a moment, Ricki stood frozen, still trying to think of something to do. Finally, she shrugged helplessly at Vanessa, mumbled a good-bye, and followed her mother.

"We should have done something!" Ricki insisted on the phone that night.

"I know," Vanessa agreed. "It happened so fast I couldn't think. But I know we could have stopped them. Things just got out of hand."

"Do you think this is the end of the tempestuous romance?" Ricki asked. "Is our parents' engagement history?"

"Oh, Ricki, that's a horrible thought. I don't know."

"Our plan down the drain." Ricki sank onto her bed pillows.

Vanessa pulled both feet into her rocker to sit cross-legged. "Even worse, I think our parents truly love each other. How sad if just one little fight . . ."

"But we were worried about this from the beginning, remember, Vee? That the differences between them would cause trouble."

"If only they could have kept on cooperating," said Vanessa, "like they were before. It seemed they were kind of ignoring the differences, don't you think?"

Ricki shrugged. "Or at least putting up with them."

Vanessa sighed. "If only your mother hadn't been late."

"Yeah. If only your dad hadn't been so touchy about it."

"Well, some people are like that," said Vanessa.

"Some people are late a lot," countered Ricki.

Vanessa frowned. "He was worried about her. She didn't call."

111

"You and your father are both worrywarts."

"You and your mother are inconsiderate sometimes," Vanessa said. "I'll admit, you've improved lately, Ricki. You've been getting more things done on time, and I know you're really putting a lot into your photography. But your mother . . . well, she's always late for dates and things with Dad."

Ricki sat up. "Wait a minute. Inconsiderate? Is it inconsiderate of my mother to offer to spend Saturday afternoon helping your father? I mean, we were there, ready to work."

"That's true. Dad overreacted, I think. He was tired."

"Mom was tired, too," Ricki said. "But she didn't lose her cool till your father started pouting. He's so irritating when he does that."

"At least he doesn't fly off the handle, like your mother does, and just storm off."

"He kicked her out!" Ricki shot back.

"No, he didn't! He suggested she go home and rest."

"He was the one who needed to rest, so that he'd stop being so crabby. I mean, he just gets so picky about things sometimes. Like last week when he yelled at me for leaving a paintbrush in the sink."

Vanessa stood up. "He absolutely did not yell at you."

"Well, I'd rather he did, than use that annoying Mr. Calm voice."

"Ricki, it was the third time you'd left the brush in the sink."

Ricki snorted. "So what? The world won't end just because I leave a stupid paintbrush in your stupid sink."

"The world might not end, but it might get as messy as your house is. Paint going down the drain pollutes the rivers."

Ricki straightened up completely. "Did you say as

112

messy as my house is? You mean because we don't pick up every little speck of dust, like you and your father do?''

"You can't even see dust at your house. It's buried under all the dirty dishes and socks and newspapers.'' Vanessa switched the phone to her other ear. The first one had gone hot with anger.

"Mom and I aren't uptight like you two are," Ricki said. "We believe in relaxing at home.''

"Ricki, your mother has probably never relaxed a day in her life. She's the uptight one. If she was wound up any tighter, she'd spin.''

"Well, how about your father, Mr. Mellow. Even when he's mad he can't let it out honestly.''

"Your mother has no trouble letting it out, does she?'' Vanessa fumed.

"I wouldn't either,'' Ricki shouted, "with a boyfriend like him!''

Vanessa put a hand on her hip. "Thanks to her temper, he may not stay her boyfriend for long.''

"Thanks to his pickiness, she won't mind that a bit.''

"Forget the Sisters Scheme,'' Vanessa said, voice trembling.

"Yeah, thanks to him.'' By now, Ricki was standing on her bed.

"Thanks to her, we'll never be sisters.''

For a few seconds they were silent, while the horrible meaning of Vanessa's words sank in.

"I'm tired of your insults," Ricki finally said.

Vanessa switched ears again. "I'm tired of yours.''

"Great. So good-bye.''

"Fine. Good-bye," replied Vanessa.

They raced to see who could hang up first.

Chapter 12

When Vanessa came through the school milk line Monday, she wasn't sure what to do.

Any other day she'd wait by the door for Ricki to come out of the lunch line. But since Saturday night, she and Ricki hadn't spoken a word to each other. They didn't talk in class or during recess that morning, and Vanessa was pretty sure they wouldn't be on speaking terms during lunch, either.

Halfheartedly Vanessa walked along the rows of tables wondering if she should sit at an empty one. She sighed. She hated fights.

As she passed one particular table she nearly dropped her milk and lunch bag. It was Courtney Haines's table, at almost the exact center of the cafeteria, where Courtney and her pals sat every day. Today, a new person sat there. Absolutely the last person anyone would ever have dreamed might sit with Courtney Haines. Ricki!

Vanessa's jaw dropped open. She couldn't stop staring.

Ricki had sandwiched herself between Paige Wallis and Heather Hurst, across the table from Courtney, who had two boys sitting next to her. Ricki took a bite of her hamburger and a gulp of soda, then said something to Courtney. And laughed. And looked up and saw Vanessa.

Vanessa blinked away as fast as she could. She kept walking.

Once in preschool, three bees had stung Vanessa at the same time on her forehead. She thought nothing else could hurt so much. But this stung, too. Without saying a word, Ricki had told her she didn't want to be friends anymore. Ricki could make friends with anyone. She obviously didn't need Vanessa or any of her other old pals.

Vanessa felt hurt, but angry, too. As she sat down at the table with Kimberly, Dani, and Louise Ann, her eyes burned with tears.

"Where's Ricki?" asked Dani.

"Sitting somewhere else," Vanessa mumbled.

"She is?" Kimberly gave Vanessa an owlish look through her big glasses.

Vanessa shrugged. "It's a free country, isn't it?"

"Vanessa." Louise Ann leaned across the table, frowning. "Are you all right? Did you two have a fight?"

Vanessa felt her eyes filling up. The tears threatened to spill over. "We're not joined at the hip, you know."

"Oh, no!" cried Dani. "This is terrible! You and Ricki, you are best friends!"

Kimberly stared, and Louise Ann frowned.

Vanessa's lower lip trembled. If her friends said just one more word, she knew she'd start crying.

Fortunately, they didn't. The last thing Vanessa wanted was for Ricki to see her cry.

The ironic part about the whole thing, Vanessa thought while nibbling on her cheese sandwich, was that her father and Ricki's mother had already made up over their argument. It had been such a silly argument, of course they'd make up. Vanessa had to admit that her argument with Ricki was silly, too. About every ten minutes afterward, she had reached for the telephone to call and apologize, then stopped herself. Sure, she had said some awful things, but she hadn't really meant them. Ricki and her mother's cleaning habits—or lack of them—did get on Vanessa's nerves, but only a little. And although Anita was late a lot and kind of nervous sometimes, she was also smart and fun and understanding, and a good mom to Ricki. Deep in her heart, Vanessa knew she'd make a good stepmother, too.

But having Anita's daughter as a stepsister, now that was a different story! Ricki had said such horrible things during their argument. *She* was the one who should apologize!

Vanessa sneaked a glance at Courtney's table, where Ricki was wadding up paper napkins and tossing them at the boys sitting next to Courtney. The boys hurled them back at her and threw extra ones at Courtney, who just giggled a lot. Everyone seemed to be having a blast with happy-go-lucky Ricki.

Fine, thought Vanessa, taking another solemn bite of her sandwich. They could have her.

Ricki lay on the cement condo balcony, peering through her camera lens at the line where the wall met the roof. She turned the camera sideways and clicked the shutter.

Mrs. McNee told her to work on perspective in her photography. That meant to look at things from different angles.

Ricki rolled onto her side and aimed at the black wrought iron bars of the railing. She was just about to snap a picture of them when a little brown bird landed on the top bar. It chirped. Ricki zoomed her lens in for a close-up shot of its gray breast and throat, then another of the underside of its beak. She had never seen the underside of a bird's beak before. Just when it was starting to get interesting, the bird decided it was scared of the shutter clicks. It took off in a flurry of feathers and chirps.

Ricki sighed, rested her camera on her chest, and crossed her arms under her head. Today it was hard to stay interested. She felt depressed. Ricki hardly ever got depressed. But how could a person not get depressed when she had just lost her best friend?

The look on Vanessa's face in the cafeteria that day appeared over and over in Ricki's mind. Vanessa's expression had been empty, as if she couldn't care less where Ricki sat at lunch.

Maybe, Ricki admitted to herself, she had taken things too far by sitting with Courtney. But she didn't want to give Vanessa a chance to snub her at their own table. If there was going to be a snub, Ricki wanted to be the one to make it.

The crummy thing was, Vanessa had snubbed her anyway. What a cold, snooty look! After that look, Ricki had started whooping it up with Courtney and company to show Vanessa what a great time she was having. But it was only a show.

All Courtney and her friends talked about was clothes, boys, and cheerleading. And after the boys got there, all the girls did was giggle! How boring. Ricki couldn't stand cheerleading. She didn't care much about clothes. And boys? Well, they were just boys.

Back in third grade, when both Courtney and Vanessa first got to Ricki's elementary school, everyone wore skateboard clothes. Courtney had about a million different colors of knee-length nylon pants. Ricki thought they looked dorky. Even if she hadn't thought so, her mother would never have bought them for her, because she was still finishing college and they were practically poor. Ricki noticed that she and the new girl, Vanessa Shepherd, were just about the only kids in third grade who didn't own sunglass headbands.

That had made Ricki feel a bond with the new girl, even though she was pretty sure that cool, pretty Vanessa would never even talk to her, the class cutup, much less be friends.

But in handwriting class one day they ended up sitting next to each other, and when Ricki got bored with making perfect cursive *B*'s, she made one into a blue elephant with a parasol that cracked Vanessa up. The two of them couldn't stop giggling. Naturally, the teacher separated them, but from then on they always played together at recess and sat together at lunch.

In those days, they had lots of fun at lunch. Today had been no fun at all.

Ricki grabbed her camera, got up, and crossed the living room to her own room. She sat on her desk, staring at the phone. Her feet spun her swivel chair around and around. For the one hundred and fiftieth time she considered picking up the phone, dialing, and saying, "Hello, Vee. This is Ricki, and I am really—"

That's where it always stopped. The most important word wouldn't come out. She absolutely could not apologize. If she did, she knew Vanessa would just act high and mighty and superior.

Ricki snorted. She gave the chair one last spin and hopped off the desk. Hmph! Let *her* call!

No sooner had she turned away than the phone rang.

Ricki dove for it. "Hello?" she asked breathlessly.

"Ricki? Hi, hon. What's the matter?"

"Oh. Hi, Mom. Nothing."

"Well, I'm afraid I'll be home a little later than usual tonight. Our staff meeting is scheduled to run long. Okay?"

"Okay," Ricki said, trying to sound normal, even

though she felt disappointed. She had been looking forward to her mom coming home, to having someone around.

Anita said, "How about pizza tomorrow night? Want to ask Vanessa?"

"Nah. She's busy."

"Oh? Doing what?"

Ricki shrugged. "I don't know. Practicing the cello or something."

"Hmm," her mom said after a pause. "Ricki, hon, you don't sound very cheerful. You didn't last night, either. Or the night before. Did you and Vanessa have an argument?"

"Yes," Ricki admitted. "So what?"

"I'm sorry to hear that. I know it can be painful to disagree with someone close to you. Can't the two of you get together and talk?" Anita asked.

"That's how we got into this fight. Talking."

Her mother paused again. "Would it be . . . nosy of me to ask—"

"Yes," Ricki interrupted. "It would."

"I thought so. It's just that I'm concerned." Anita's voice sounded tense.

"About what?" asked Ricki. "That your daughter is having a fight with your boyfriend's daughter?"

Anita laughed. "I guess that sizes it up. But Ricki, hon, Andy isn't just my boyfriend. He's more than that to me. He's . . ."

Suddenly Ricki realized what her mother's worried tone meant. "Mom, do you have something to tell me?"

"Well, we'll talk tonight, hon. I'll be home at—"

"Wait," Ricki said. "Mom, you . . . you and Andy

have decided, haven't you? He's not your boyfriend. He's—"

Silence.

"He's your fiancé!"

"I wanted to tell you in person, sweetie," her mother finally said. "I had planned on it tonight, but . . ."

Ricki sat speechless. This was amazing. Her dream—and Vanessa's—had come true. The Sisters Scheme had worked!

She remembered something she'd heard once, an old saying: Be careful what you wish for. You might get it.

"Let's just talk to the minister, Anita, since we already have the appointment."

"Oh, Andy, I don't know. I'm just not sure."

The two of them stood at the altar of one of the biggest churches Vanessa had ever seen. Their voices echoed off the distant walls. Vanessa sat in a pew on one side of the church and Ricki sat on the other while their parents debated.

"So you don't have your heart set on this church for the wedding?" Andy asked, hands in jeans pockets.

"Well, no." Anita fiddled with the collar of her gray trench coat. "It just seemed like such a nice place when I saw it the first time. Very inspiring."

"Which you decided when you attended a funeral here," Andy pointed out.

"So you don't like it," Anita shot back.

"No, I do." Andy gazed up at the three-story-high domed ceiling. "It's . . . it's majestic."

"And cold," Anita added.

"No, I'm not cold," said Andy.

"I mean the atmosphere." Anita rubbed her arms. "Gloomy, isn't it?"

"Well, it's not the most festive building in the world." Andy nodded, stroking his brown beard.

Vanessa couldn't agree more. The church was gloomy. Lots of dark gray marble, maroon carpeting, and silver trimmings everywhere, plus a musty, smoky smell. That morning when her father asked her to come look at a church Anita had in mind for the wedding, Vanessa imagined something small and sunny and colorful. A place to celebrate. Although she wondered if she would feel like celebrating in time for the wedding two months away, considering the fact that she and her future stepsister were still not on speaking terms.

Spring vacation from school had started soon after their argument, making it all the easier not to see each other. Now, on Saturday, Ricki and Vanessa hadn't talked in seven days—a record.

Vanessa hated it.

Yesterday she had come within inches of calling Ricki. It was while packing her room for the move. Her father had asked if she could be ready in two weeks, and she had agreed right away. But no matter how excited a person might be about moving (and Vanessa had to admit, she had gotten pretty excited), that person couldn't help feeling sad about leaving the place where she had lived for three years.

While she wrapped her miniature ceramic horses in newspaper, Vanessa's new enthusiasm about living on Mariposa Lane felt kind of hollow, because Ricki wasn't there to share it. After all, Ricki was the one who had listened to her worries about the new house, who had helped her see the good part about moving. Nowadays, Vanessa was planning just how she would arrange her furniture in her new room overlooking the backyard.

But with every book and sock that went into the boxes,

Vanessa felt more lonely. The feeling got even worse after she heard Marlys and Mavis calling to her from outside.

"Hi!" she shouted back from the window. "Want to come up?"

"We can't," said Marlys. "Mavis has gymnastics."

Marlys couldn't be in gymnastics because she had bad asthma, but she always went to Mavis's classes anyway to watch. The twins rarely went anywhere without each other.

Vanessa felt a fresh pang of missing Ricki. She sighed and propped her elbows on the windowsill. As Mavis and Marlys walked away, she noticed they wore identical green plaid pants and yellow turtleneck shirts. Identical green plastic headbands held back their clouds of auburn curls. They even walked in step, at exactly the same pace, with little Murphy trotting along beside them.

Part of Vanessa felt jealous. They never had to be lonely or sad. They always had each other. But another part of her wondered if she would really want to be like that, almost identical to someone else. Look alike, walk alike, think alike?

Vanessa couldn't imagine being much like Ricki. The two of them were opposites in so many ways. Well, the *Love Guide* had said opposites attract. People are drawn to others for qualities they themselves lack. Life was probably more interesting that way, Vanessa decided. And maybe that was one reason why she and Ricki had made such good friends.

But the *Love Guide* also said people could be too different from each other. Were she and Ricki just too different to stay friends? Or, to become good sisters?

Thoughts coming back to the present, Vanessa peeked across the church aisle at the girl who was very soon to become her sister, like it or not. Ricki wore a pinched, ugly look on her face, as if she had just eaten something sour.

Obviously, Ricki didn't want to be sisters with her, Vanessa decided. Nor did Ricki want Andy for a step-father. Maybe she didn't like the church, either.

Ricki sneezed.

Vanessa fixed her eyes on her lap, feeling sadder than ever. There they were in a church with their parents, who were standing at the altar and planning their upcoming wedding. It should have been one of the happiest moments of their lives.

Ricki sneezed again.

Forcing herself not to cry, Vanessa drew a deep breath. If only she and Ricki could be friends again!

A third sneeze.

Vanessa sneaked a glance at Ricki, whose nose wrinkled up and eyes watered. Her chest puffed in and out as if she were fighting off another sneeze. But she couldn't. The sneeze came anyway—the loudest of all.

"Honey? What is it?" Anita came down the aisle toward her.

Ricki shook her head. "I. Don't. Know. *Achoo!* Maybe the . . . *Achoo!*"

Andy followed Anita to stand by Ricki's side.

Ricki's shoulders hunched forward. Her breathing came in wheezes. "I think . . ." She sneezed again. "It's . . . that smell."

"The incense?" Anita asked.

Ricki managed to nod. "It . . . makes my nose itch."

Vanessa saw Anita give Andy a hopeless look. It seemed to say, "See? This place is not meant for us."

Andy nodded and said to Ricki, "Come on. Let's get you outside."

He and Anita guided Ricki down the aisle amid a small storm of more sneezes. Vanessa followed.

Anita pushed open the heavy church door, letting in a blustery wind from outside.

"Oh!" she cried. "Let's get you into the car, honey. It's a mess out here."

Andy unlocked a back door of his old green van and helped Ricki in. "How're you doing?"

Ricki took a breath and nodded. "Better, I think. I still have to—*achoo!*—sneeze, but my nose doesn't itch so much now."

"You must have been allergic to something in there." Anita frowned, her curls flattened to her head by the wind.

Vanessa buttoned her sweater. "I'm getting blown away. Are we leaving now?"

"Oh, sorry, Vee," Andy said. "Why don't you get in with Ricki and wait while Anita and I talk with the minister. We won't be long."

Through the car doorway Ricki saw Vanessa's stony expression. "I can stay alone," she said in between blowing her nose.

"No," Anita said. "You two stay in the car for a minute. Just lock the doors. The church office is right there. We'll keep an eye on you out the window."

Anita and Andy shot looks at each other. Ricki wasn't sure, but she thought she saw her mother wink.

Chapter 13

Vanessa got in on the opposite side of the backseat from Ricki. She shut the door and locked it, then gave her father's back a scowl as he walked away with Anita.

Vanessa's dad knew she and Ricki weren't talking. He hadn't said much about it earlier, but now he and Anita probably thought they were sly ones, making her and Ricki stay alone together.

Ricki blew her nose.

Then came a long, stiff silence.

Ricki was the first to speak. "You can go in there with them if you want. I wouldn't mind waiting alone."

"Dad said I have to stay," Vanessa answered in a monotone voice.

Ricki sniffed loudly. "Don't do it for my sake."

"Don't worry, I won't."

"Right. I'm sure you wouldn't."

Vanessa pursed her lips. "What's that supposed to mean?"

Ricki shrugged, then climbed halfway into the front seat to grab fresh tissues from a box on the dashboard.

Vanessa stared out at the wind swirling up dust and trash.

"Yakoo dent carlesh," Ricki said through the tissue.

Vanessa frowned at her. "What?"

Another nose blow, then Ricki muttered, "You couldn't care less."

"Me? I couldn't care less? You're the one who—" Vanessa stopped herself. She absolutely refused to get into another argument.

Ricki went through a half-dozen more tissues before she was able to draw a clear breath. She sighed in relief. Then she started fidgeting. Her mother and Andy still sat with the minister. She could see them through the office window, talking. She felt miserable. Nothing was going right, just nothing! She and Vanessa couldn't even talk without starting a fight. Their parents couldn't find a place to get married. And incense made her nose itch. Now the car windows were getting foggy.

She opened her door.

"Where are you going?" Vanessa demanded.

The wind whipped at Ricki's pile of used tissues. "To get some fresh air."

"Dad said to stay in the car."

"I don't have to do whatever your father says," Ricki flung back, hanging onto the door to keep it from blowing off its hinges. Then she bit her tongue. No more arguing.

"Please shut it," Vanessa said.

Ricki tapped her fingers on the door's handle for a few seconds, then pulled it shut with a slam. She slumped in the seat, hands jammed deep into the pockets of her overalls.

The windows got foggier. Gusts of wind blew so hard at the van that it shook.

"Thank you," Vanessa said.

Ricki frowned at her suspiciously. "For what?"

"For shutting the door."

"Oh. You're welcome." Ricki fidgeted more, then began to print her name in large letters in her window fog.

Vanessa chewed on her cheek. Her father did not like people drawing in the window fog. It left streaks and smudges that were hard to clean. But she didn't say so to Ricki. Instead, she took a breath and asked, "Are you feeling better?"

Ricki drew little circles over the *i*'s in her name. "Yes." She stuffed her hands back in her pockets. "Thank you. Go inside if you want to. You don't have to stay just to take care of me."

Vanessa raised an eyebrow. "Do you want me to leave?"

Ricki shrugged. "They're taking a long time."

The girl's saw their parents and the minister laughing. "They seem to be enjoying themselves," Vanessa said.

Ricki mumbled, "They're really going to do it."

"Do what?"

"Get married."

"You've just realized that?" Vanessa asked.

"It was supposed to be different." Ricki sniffed.

The sniff sounded odd to Vanessa. Longer and heavier than the others. She dared a glance at Ricki.

Ricki met her eyes. "Really different."

Vanessa nodded. "We—we were supposed to be happy about it."

"Are you happy?" Ricki asked.

"Are you?"

"I asked you first."

Vanessa shrugged a shoulder. "*They're* happy."

"Yeah. Lovebirds. Great idea we had."

"It worked," Vanessa said.

Ricki caught half a smile on Vanessa's face. She smiled, too, just a little. "We sure did a good job."

"Well, it was your idea," said Vanessa.

"It was? No, it wasn't. It was yours."

127

Vanessa shook her head. "You thought of it."

"No way," Ricki insisted. "You're the one who thought it would be so great if they got married."

"Well, so did you. Nobody forced you to work on the Sisters Scheme." She thrust her chin forward stubbornly.

Ricki narrowed her eyes. "Hey, wait a minute—"

Vanessa put her hands over her ears.

"What are you doing?" Ricki wanted to know.

"I don't want to argue anymore," muttered Vanessa.

Ricki sighed. "How come we've been fighting so much?"

Vanessa's lower lip began to tremble. "Maybe we're scared."

"Would you please take your hands off your ears? Scared of what?"

"I don't know." Vanessa let her hands drop. "Of not being best friends anymore."

Ricki frowned. "Of being sisters, instead of best friends."

"Maybe," Vanessa said, reaching for Ricki's tissue box, "if we're sisters, we won't be best friends anymore."

"Vee." Ricki bunched her mouth to one side. "I'm sorry."

Vanessa let a breath out. "Oh, me, too. I—I missed you."

"I missed you, too," Ricki said.

Vanessa grabbed a tissue. "I feel like crying."

"Me, too."

"What? You never cry." Vanessa eyed her.

"Sure I do. Here, I'll show you." Ricki sniffled.

"Oh, that's just left over from your sneezing fit."

"Boo-hoo," wailed Ricki in a whiny voice. "Oh, boo-hoo-hoo."

"Cut it out." Grinning, Vanessa gave her a shove.

"Boo-hoo." Ricki crammed her face into a tissue. "Boo—"

"Aahh!" Both girls jumped at once when the van door suddenly flew open.

"Ricki? Are you all right?" Andy leaned in with a worried frown.

Ricki recovered from the scare first. "Oh. Fine. I'm fine."

"But you're still sneezing, honey," her mother said. "Maybe we should see the doctor."

"I was just, um, blowing my nose," Ricki said.

Anita stroked Ricki's bangs away from her eyes. "Well, we asked the minister about the sneezing, and he said they've been using a new brand of incense in the church. A lot of people are having reactions, so they're changing it."

"Oh," Vanessa said. "Then does that mean . . ."

"Does that mean what?" Andy got into the driver's seat.

"That you'll have the wedding here?" Vanessa asked.

Anita settled into the front seat and sighed. "We really like the Reverend Polaski. But it just doesn't seem quite right for us here. It's such a big church for our small guest list."

"But we're having trouble finding alternatives," Andy said. "Most churches and halls and even parks are already booked for weddings in June."

Vanessa shrugged. "Well, our house isn't."

Ricki turned to look at her. So did Anita and Andy.

"Huh?" Andy said.

"Our new house. It would be just the right size. And it's not gloomy."

Andy and Anita traded glances.

"Yeah," said Ricki, "I bet the house will look really great in June. All the flowers in bloom, lots of sunshine . . ."

"Hmm." Andy eyed the girls in the rearview mirror.

"Hmm," echoed Anita, smiling. "Have you been plotting this?"

"Are you two, um, friendly again?" asked Andy.

"Everyone has their disagreements." Vanessa looked pointedly at both adults.

"Anyway," Ricki cut in, "the house will be in great shape by June, won't it?"

"It could be," Andy agreed.

"Andy, hon, I think Vanessa's idea could turn out to be a wonderful one," said Anita.

Andy grinned back at her like a little boy on Christmas morning. "You would really consider marrying me in that old shack?"

"Oh, hon," Anita took his hand. "You know I love the house. But how would you feel about it?"

Andy beamed, doing a terrible job of hiding his excitement. "I think it could be arranged."

"The girls are right," Anita said. "It would be so lovely there. And so . . . sweet. A combination wedding and housewarming."

Andy kissed her hand.

Ricki rolled her eyes, and Vanessa giggled, just as they usually did these days whenever their parents got mushy.

"It'll be more than a wedding and more than a housewarming," Andy said. He grinned at Vanessa and Ricki, still holding Anita's hand. "It will be a *family* warming."

Chapter 14

Ricki squirmed. Her white nylon panty hose itched. The stiff collar of her ruffled yellow dress choked her.

Vanessa whispered, "Are you going to do that all day?"

"Do what?"

"Scratch your knees and make faces."

"I can't help it," Ricki said. "I'm uncomfortable. I wouldn't wear this stuff for any other occasion, you know. Except maybe to meet the president or somebody. Maybe."

On the backyard patio, Vanessa and Ricki arranged the last of the flowers that Andy's artist friend Maureen had brought for the arched bower that another artist, Bernard, had built for the wedding.

"At least you look good in this kind of outfit," Ricki went on.

Vanessa wore yellow, too—a lace-collared dress that swirled to below her knees. Small and graceful, she seemed to belong in it.

"Me?" Vanessa pointed at herself. "But I'm pale and short, and I fade into the wallpaper," Vanessa complained. "You've got a year-round tan, and you're tall and self-assured. . . ."

Ricki rolled her eyes. "Give me a break."

Soon the bower was completely covered with yellow roses and white daisies woven in with English ivy. Around the patio, rows of chairs had been draped with long white ribbons by Ricki's aunts. The members of Fast Forward tuned their instruments on the deck off the kitchen, and inside the kitchen Uncle Mario was putting last touches on the Mexican feast he had prepared for the reception. Guests milled around, sipping punch or the French champagne that Vanessa's grandparents had sent.

Vanessa sighed. It was all going perfectly. Too perfectly.

"Ricki," she said as they gave the chairs a last-minute check for bugs. "Why are we so calm?"

"What time is it?" Ricki asked.

Vanessa looked at her watch. "Three thirty-seven."

"That explains it. In exactly twenty-three minutes our lives will change forever. Why shouldn't we be totally calm and cool?" Ricki made a goofy cross-eyed face. "Vee, do you feel calm?"

"Not a bit. Do you?"

"I'm petrified."

Vanessa nodded. "That's why we seem calm. We're too terrified even to act nervous."

"I am nervous," Ricki said.

"So am I." Vanessa chewed on her cheek.

Ricki brushed a leaf off a chair.

"Ricki, there's nothing to worry about. Everything is fine. It's all ready. What could possibly go wrong?" Vanessa asked.

"Nothing. Except, oh, earthquake, rainstorm . . ." Ricki listed.

"No, we've already had one of each of those."

"True," Ricki agreed. "And our parents can't have another argument at this point, can they?"

"Gosh, I hope not. They've had three just in the past week! Oh, Ricki, what if—"

"Vee, they can't. Look, your dad is right over there chatting with the Reverend Polaski and my grandpa. And my mom is upstairs with Grandma and my aunts finishing her hair. Our parents are not going to see each other again until Mom is walking up that aisle. Grandma said she'd make sure of it. She's superstitious."

Vanessa sighed. "Okay, okay. Enough worrying."

"Right." Ricki chewed on her thumbnail.

"Ricki?"

"What?"

"Did you remember your toothbrush?" Vanessa asked.

"Yeah. It's in my suitcase."

"Good, because my Great Aunt Allegra is going to make us brush our teeth three times a day while our parents are on their honeymoon."

"Three times a day!" Ricki widened her eyes.

Vanessa nodded. "She's like that."

"Hey, I thought you said this was going to be a great month! That Great Aunt Allegra is really nice and sweet."

"She is really nice and sweet. You met her. But she once illustrated a children's book about dental care, and— Ricki, what are you grinning about?"

"Oh, just thinking. That I've got a few relatives for *you*. I mean, now that they're going to be yours, too. There's my second cousin Duke over there talking to Gordon. He's from Iowa and can imitate the Canada goose. He does it often."

"The Canada goose?" Vanessa echoed.

"And then there's my Aunt Beatrice. She believes that aliens kidnapped her for a day, but they were really nice and only hypnotized her so that they could read her astral aura.''

Vanessa raised an eyebrow. "Oh. I can hardly wait. Well, share and share alike, as they say."

Ricki giggled. "What's mine is yours!"

"You know." Vanessa sighed again. "It was less than a year ago that we were only dreaming about this. Seems like forever!"

"We stood right out there where the weeds used to be, and you were about to cry 'cause—"

"Ricki, don't say you told me so."

"Okay, but you did hate this place."

"I didn't hate it. I felt . . . doubtful."

"You said if I lived here with you it would be okay. But I think you would have ended up liking it anyway." Ricki grinned.

Vanessa shrugged a shoulder and smiled. "I guess it's not so bad. And now you *are* going to live here with us!"

"I can hardly believe it! When the lovebirds come back from their honeymoon and Mom and I move in with all our stuff, I guess it'll seem more real."

"I think so, too. Oh, here comes Dad!"

"He looks really handsome," Ricki whispered.

Andy wore a gray suit and a silky white tie, along with the biggest, happiest grin Ricki had ever seen. Kissing both girls on the forehead, he asked, "Are the maid of honor and the best man ready?"

"I wish you wouldn't call me that, Dad," Vanessa said. "How about best . . ."

"Person," Ricki offered.

"Best person! Yes," agreed Vanessa. Then she looked at her watch. "Oh, it's almost time!"

"Really? Is it?" Ricki grabbed Vanessa's wrist. "Three fifty-four. Oh, my gosh! Only six minutes!"

"Hey." Andy laughed. "You two aren't nervous, are you?"

"Us?" they asked in unison.

Andy laughed again, hugging them both to his sides.

Mrs. Quan waddled up and snapped a picture. "Oh, so nice!"

Andy helped Mrs. Quan and the other guests to their seats, then motioned to the girls to join him under the bower. Suzanne came up and handed Vanessa a bouquet of yellow jonquils.

"Oh, they're perfect!" Vanessa cried, kissing her.

The band played "It Had To Be You," a soft, romantic song that Ricki and Vanessa had watched their parents slow dance to in the living room a few nights ago.

Standing beside her dad, Vanessa whispered to Ricki, "Two more minutes!"

Ricki waited on the other side of the bower for her mother. She scratched her knees. The more nervous she got, the more the dumb stockings itched. It was hard to scratch and hold her maid of honor bouquet at the same time.

Off to the side, Uncle Mario gave her the thumbs-up sign from behind his video camera. He had promised to take plenty of regular pictures, too. In the front row, Grandpa, Aunt Ruth, and Aunt Marie tried to keep the little cousins quiet. Aunt Laura blew Ricki a kiss. With tears in her eyes, Grandma whispered to her in Spanish that she looked beautiful.

Ricki grinned back and tried to stop scratching. But what if something did happen at the last minute to ruin everything?

Her eyes fell on Milton, the nerdy guy from her mother's office who used to have a crush on Anita. What if, at the point where the minister said that anyone who might object to the wedding should speak now or forever hold their peace, Milton stood up and spoke?

Ricki swallowed. She glanced at Vanessa for courage. That was no help. Vanessa was chewing on her cheek.

Suddenly the band broke off the song and started playing a jazzy version of "The Wedding March." Then Anita appeared in the doorway of the house in her short, peach-colored dress, positively glowing.

Ricki forgot all about her itchy stockings. Vanessa breathed a deep, relieved sigh. They both glanced up at Andy, who looked as if he had just seen heaven.

And just at that moment, Great Aunt Allegra tottered into the aisle. "Pardon me!" she called in her old, shaky voice. "Oh, I do beg your pardon."

The music stopped.

Great Aunt Allegra tottered right up to Vanessa, balancing on her cane like a little bird on a wind-licked twig. "My dear," she whispered, fixing Vanessa with her huge blue eyes. "I am terribly sorry. But the doorbell rang, and I presumed to answer. This just arrived. Addressed to you." She held out a small yellow envelope.

"A telegram," Andy murmured.

Vanessa's fingers trembled as she tore the envelope's flap. Could it be from her grandparents? Papa had a bad cold, but Nona would call if anything serious happened, wouldn't she?

TO VANESSA SHEPHERD, it read. BEST WISHES TODAY, SWEETHEART. MISS YOU. STILL IN ISLANDS. WILL VISIT SOON. LOVE. MAMA.

"Vee," Ricki whispered. Vanessa had gone white as a ghost. Ricki looked from her to Andy. "What is it?"

Vanessa handed the telegram to her father. He scanned it, sighed heavily, then managed a grin.

Vanessa sighed, too, and finally whispered to Ricki, "It's aloha. From Hawaii."

"Oh!" Ricki told her heart to stop pounding. Then she rolled her eyes. What a time for a telegram from Vanessa's mom!

"Is everything all right?" Anita called from down the aisle.

"Just fine!" Vanessa called back.

"Yeah, honey, just fine," Andy added.

Gordon played a little fanfare on his keyboard for punctuation. The guests all laughed.

"Shall we begin?" asked the Reverend Polaski.

"Yeah, please do!" Ricki answered.

More chuckles from the guests. Then the band started up "The Wedding March" again.

Vanessa tucked the telegram into her dress pocket. Leave it to her mother for timing! No letter for over two months, then this! And as far as timing went, Great Aunt Allegra should be on Celeste's side of the family instead of Andy's. Well, maybe her mom's visit would be timed better. Although with Celeste, you never knew.

Vanessa took a breath. At that moment, the most important thing was that Ricki's mother was walking down the aisle toward her dad, eyes glistening with happiness. After just a few more minutes, a hundred telegrams could come, and it wouldn't matter. Her father and Ricki's mother would be married! Finally! And finally, she and Ricki would be . . .

Sisters! Ricki was saying to herself over and over. She was so excited she could hardly keep still.

Anita took her place beside Andy and gave Ricki her bouquet to hold, along with a little hug. Ricki hugged her

137

ck and had to fight off a sniffle. What a time to feel like crying!

As Anita and Andy moved together and took each other's hands, the minister began the ceremony.

The girls' eyes met across the flower-decked bower. Vanessa winked. Ricki winked back. And under their bouquets, they both kept their fingers crossed.